THE NURSE'S HOMECOMING

BOOK 2 IN THE VICTORIA'S WAR SERIES

FENELLA J MILLER

First published in 2015 as Victoria's War: Reunited. This edition first published in Great Britain in 2024 by Boldwood Books Ltd.

Cover Design by Colin Thomas

Cover Photography: Colin Thomas and Alamy

A CIP catalogue record for this book is available from the British Library.

Paperback ISBN 978-1-83518-672-5

Large Print ISBN 978-1-83518-673-2

Hardback ISBN 978-1-83518-671-8

Ebook ISBN 978-1-83518-674-9

Kindle ISBN 978-1-83518-675-6

Audio CD ISBN 978-1-83518-666-4

MP3 CD ISBN 978-1-83518-667-1

Digital audio download ISBN 978-1-83518-670-1

Boldwood Books Ltd
23 Bowerdean Street
London SW6 3TN
www.boldwoodbooks.com

In memory of my mother, Patrica Cross, nee Rikh, whose memoirs inspired this book.

AUTHOR'S NOTE

The characters in this story are an accurate reflection of the time they are living in. As such, their thoughts, speech and actions are normal for this era. Thankfully we now live in a more enlightened time.

PART I

INDIA 1944

1

THE BIG PUSH

First Lieutenant Victoria Jones had no time to think about the implications of what her parents had told her during the far too brief time they had spent together at the Raj Hotel in Madras. Until the war was over she must concentrate on the job in hand – that of being a nurse on the Burma front. Time enough to consider her options when she was demobbed. Until then she would be just a nurse in the QAs and not the Anglo-Indian daughter of the Rajah of Marpur, the widow of a Dunkirk hero, or the woman who had abandoned her four-year-old child to the care of her grandparents.

She inhaled the unmistakable aroma of the jungle

and, unlike her fellow nurses, revelled in the damp, fetid smell and the overpowering heat. Despite the racket from the battered aeroplane from which they had just emerged taxiing to its take-off position, the familiar sound of screeching monkeys and exotic birds was clearly audible from the dense jungle that surrounded the primitive airstrip.

No doubt they would have to hang about in the stifling heat for an hour or two before anyone came to collect them. Their boxes and bags had been dumped unceremoniously by the corrugated iron shed that functioned as a reception area and headquarters. No one had come out to greet them and they slumped in wilting heaps on their boxes. Even Nester, famous for her complaining, was silent for a change.

Enid, although she had only known her a few days, had already become a chum. 'I could do with a pee but I'm not sure I have the energy to look for the latrine. I suppose I had better make the effort. It might be some time before we get a chance to go.'

'There's a lean-to over there – I think that might be it. Anyone else coming?' Victoria glanced at her companions but they were too exhausted and dispirited to do more than shake their heads. 'Right, Enid, just you and me then.'

Although the stench in the latrine was thick

enough to cut, the relief of emptying her bladder more than made up for the unpleasant experience. She and Enid emerged from the lean-to see the others were on their feet and waving madly.

The transport was arriving to take them on the final leg of the journey and this comprised of two American jeeps. There was no room for the precious luggage so it was thrown into the back of an old ambulance as the group piled into the other vehicles.

'I think one of us should travel with our luggage. Anyone volunteering?' Valerie, a major and in charge of their party, asked hopefully. Instantly Victoria jumped down.

'I'll do it. I know the ambulance is more likely to get stuck, but at least when it rains I shall be dryer than you lot.'

'Good egg, Jones. We'll keep your holdall and things and stake you a claim in a tent,' Enid shouted as the two jeeps shot off down the track, leaving her to run back and scramble into the front seat of the ambulance before it left without her.

The driver was an NCO of indeterminate age and grudging humour. She decided it would be best not to engage him in conversation; after all, officers and the ranks were not supposed to fraternise. The tracks they followed into the jungle were well defined, obviously in frequent use by other larger vehicles. Despite the persistent heavy rain over the past few days, they made reasonable progress. The only point of concern was when they arrived at a bridge over a swollen river that had been widened by the addition of several wooden planks. She was tempted to ask if she could get out and walk across, but decided it would seem weak-kneed to do so.

The driver acknowledged her presence for the first time. 'Hang on, ma'am, it's do or die.' She braced herself, grabbing the strap attached to the door, and closed her eyes to send up a quick prayer. The driver released the clutch, put his foot down and they thundered across the bridge in one piece.

'Are there many more like that before we get there?'

'Two, but neither as dodgy as this one. A lorry fell in the day before yesterday and the Yanks had to pull it out with one of their cranes. A good job they've got the equipment because we bloody haven't.'

The news that the Americans were functioning deep in the jungle gave her a feeling of security. Captain Taylor King, the rangy American she had met briefly on the train, was out here somewhere. Although they had only spent half an hour together, she had a feeling he was going to be important to her – that is if he ever found her in the jungle.

The old ambulance slowed down to negotiate a sharp bend and then shuddered to a halt. She looked around in surprise. Wherever it was, she had arrived. There was no sign of the two jeeps.

'Are you sure this is the right place? We didn't pass the jeeps and they should have been here before us.'

The man removed his hat and scratched his balding head. 'Buggered if I know, ma'am. I reckon that a mile or so back they went right instead of left. It's bleeding difficult to turn round up there, but they'll manage. Those four-wheel drives, they can go anywhere.'

She got down and looked around and her mouth dropped. Where on earth was she? This was little more than a clearing in the jungle. There was a wide dish-shaped depression in the ground with tracks leading off in all directions. The steep sides were a tangle of green, apart from on the far edge where two ropes had been tied either side of a well-worn path that led over the top of the bowl's edge.

Strangely there were the burnt-out remains of two aircraft, so there must have been a landing strip here at one time. She shuddered. How quickly the undergrowth had reclaimed it. Apart from these there were a few tents, a couple of Nissen huts, piles of equipment, but little else.

The only occupants of the clearing were three shirtless soldiers all with enormous bushy beards. Instead of greeting her with delight she heard one of them swear volubly and turn to his companion in disgust.

'We'll have to put bloody screens around the bloody latrines now. What the hell do they want to send women here for?'

She didn't find this remark at all amusing; in fact she agreed with him. What possible use could a group of highly skilled and competent nurses be in the middle of nowhere? Before she could form an opinion a harassed-looking major hurried over from one of the more solid-looking structures to greet her.

'Welcome, Lieutenant, we have been expecting you. There's a big push about to start and we want you to set up a field hospital here.' He gestured vaguely around the clearing. 'All the equipment you'll need is up there. I'll send you a team of men but you must organise them to bring it down.'

Victoria finally recovered the power of speech. 'A hospital? Where exactly are we?'

The man grinned. 'This is Imphal, Lieutenant. No doubt you've heard about us.'

Indeed she had. While she'd been in Colombo the news had been full of little else. "*There was grave concern that the survivors at Imphal... Battle raged around Imphal... The road to Imphal had been cut.*" In fact, it had seldom been out of the news. Why on earth would anyone wish to fight over this place?

'Thank you, sir, you can leave it to me. As soon as the porters arrive I'll get our boxes and things unloaded from the ambulance. Did you have a particular spot in mind for the hospital or is that up to me as well?'

'Point taken, Lieutenant. I tell you what; I haven't the foggiest idea where the MO wants it. You get your stuff out of that ambulance and pile it up somewhere, and let's pray it doesn't rain for a bit. I should steer well clear of the latrines if I was you.'

She could have made that decision for herself – the stench wafting across was unmistakable and decidedly unpleasant.

When the rest of her travelling companions arrived two hours later, she had everything under control. Being able to speak the language had meant she had no difficulty giving her instructions and there was now a constant string of loinclothed men running up the steep hill empty-handed and back down carrying various bits of vital equipment. They didn't use the ropes attached to the slope to assist them.

The medical officer, Major Rhodes, had turned up and together they'd scratched out the site for the field hospital, and after that it was simple. She had to check the labels on the boxes and cases as they arrived and get them stacked in the correct space. All that remained to do was get the men to begin erecting the tents and assembling the camp furniture.

Valerie looked decidedly disgruntled that her role as commanding officer had been usurped in her absence. 'I say, Victoria, what's going on here?'

'This is Imphal, Valerie, and we're here to set up a field hospital. There's going to be a big push any day now and there will be casualties pouring in. Major Rhodes, the MO, and I marked out the spaces for the operating theatres, the wards, and so on. I've put our boxes over there; it looks as though we're sleeping on-site as well.'

Enid was impressed. 'Golly, you've been busy. Whilst we've been wandering around like lambs in the wilderness you've arranged a field hospital single-handedly. What do you want us to do now?'

Victoria felt Valerie's resentment pouring over her and for a split second hesitated. 'Right, Enid, if you and Angela could get the men to put up our tents over there, and once they're up get the boxes in the right places. Betty, if you take three others and this list and just check that all the equipment the MO told me was coming is actually there.' She turned to Valerie. 'Valerie, let me bring you up to speed. You are the CO, so you've got to take over from here. You'll need to know exactly what's going on first.'

Whatever else she was, Valerie was a good nurse and a better soldier. Victoria watched her swallow her anger. 'Right. Fire away, I'm all ears. I must say, Jones, you've done a splendid job. Couldn't have done better myself.'

She snapped to attention and saluted smartly. 'Thank you, ma'am.' Harmony restored, they got on with setting up the temporary field hospital.

* * *

Within three days everything was ready and an anaesthetist and another doctor had been flown in to join them. They now had three wards, each made up of a cluster of tents. There were six camp beds in each tent, and each ward had an open-sided marquee for the nurses to store drugs and equipment in and be able to discuss procedures out of the earshot of the patients.

Accommodation was primitive, with hand-dug latrines and makeshift showers, which only worked when it was raining. Hot water was brought down the steep slope twice a day, but there never was enough to do more than a strip wash.

There was now a lull and Major Rhodes told them they could have a couple of days' R & R before things kicked off. The track up the side of the site was slippery and without the assistance of the ropes none of them would have made it to the top without getting covered in mud.

Victoria had made this ascent many times already, but most of the others hadn't. Enid looked around.

'Good God! This is not much better than down there; there's just more of it and it's a bit more permanent-looking.'

'Never mind, the major said there are hot showers and decent food – that's good enough for me.' Valerie marched off, towel and washbag under her arm, and the rest of them scurried after her.

The injured began to arrive shortly after they returned from their brief stay in the hillside camp. Victoria had been put in charge of her ward; Enid was her deputy. They were on duty virtually twenty-four hours a day, snatching short spells to sleep whenever they could. Her ward was used for post-operative recuperation. Only the most severe injuries came to her and Enid. Many of the young men died and every one was mourned. She had no idea where the battle was being fought but knew the front line was deep in the jungle. The distinctive whump-whump of the mortars and the fighter planes screaming overhead were a constant accompaniment, so it couldn't be far away. It appeared all this action was to reopen the road – again.

The Japanese were being driven slowly back by the tenacity of the British Forces and the accuracy of the RAF and American fighter planes. Six weeks after their arrival the last of the patients were driven away and the field hospital was defunct.

Major Rhodes called them together for a debrief. 'Well done, ladies and gentlemen. I have been informed by the higher-ups that our efforts have been appreciated but we're no longer needed here. All we have to do now is pack up and get everything back on the lorries. The front is moving forward and so must the field hospital.'

She was not the only one to feel dismay. After working non-stop for six weeks she had been hoping she might get at least get a week off to recuperate before being sent deeper into the jungle.

'Don't look so worried – you're being given a

week's R & R. There's not a lot to do round here, but there's an American base about an hour's drive away and they've got all the luxuries we haven't. They're expecting your arrival later today.' He beamed at them, delighted his good news was appreciated. 'You'll be shipped from there to wherever we set up the next hospital. See you in ten days or so. Enjoy your rest – you've earned it.' He saluted and they returned the gesture.

'An American base? Coca-Cola and candy, hot showers and silk stockings, and generous GIs – what more could a lady want?'

'Trust you, Angela, to think of men! What I want is to be clean and sleep in a dry bed.'

Victoria agreed with Betty – it would be wonderful to sleep somewhere without the constant drip of water on one's bedding. For the past six weeks none of them had been dry. They were all suffering from a variety of fungal conditions and foot rot.

* * *

The Americans had done more than throw up a few tents in a clearing; they had built what was almost a small town. Clutching her holdall and tin hat, and with her haversack slung over one shoulder, Victoria gazed around in awe.

'Blimey, how could they build all this out here?' Enid said.

'They're Yanks, Enid, they can do anything; they've got the resources we haven't,' Valerie told her.

They had scarcely disembarked from the lorry before two GIs trotted across to greet them. They saluted sloppily and stood grinning down at them. These men were clean and well fed; a stark contrast to the servicemen they'd been dealing with.

'Hi, good afternoon. It's just swell to see you. We've got everything laid on, best accommodation, good food, and plenty of rest.'

The speaker, a young man, his blond crew cut gleaming in the watery sunlight, led them down the main street and past a large building. 'This is the officers' mess. You'll need your glad rags on tonight; they're putting on a big party for you. Our guys have heard all about your work down there on the front, and we sure appreciate what you did for our buddies.'

Victoria was puzzled by this. As far as she knew they'd only treated British servicemen. 'I don't think we treated any Americans; it was all British personnel. I expect you've got your own excellent facilities somewhere else.'

'I guess one wounded soldier looks very much like another, ma'am. I'm sure you didn't stop to ask their names. I know at least six of my buddies came through your hospital, and they've all been shipped home alive. It wouldn't have happened without you being there working your butts off.'

The darker, Mediterranean-looking GI, pointed to a row of wooden buildings on the far side of the compound. 'That's where the GIs bunk. The officers have the large building at the far end. You ladies are here; this place is kept for VIPs.'

Two privates were waiting at the door of their temporary home. They were saluted in, and left to their own devices.

'Golly, this is posh,' Enid said. 'This must be the recreation room, so there has to be a dormitory somewhere else.'

They explored the large building and to their delight discovered they were two to a room, and as Victoria had hoped, there were real beds and cotton sheets to sleep between.

'The showers are huge, and there's four of them, and two baths and four WCs. We won't want to go out – this is like the Ritz.'

'Hardly that, Enid, but it will certainly make a very welcome change from where we've been for the past few weeks.' Valerie, as expected, selected her room first.

As far as Victoria could see there was little to distinguish between them, and she was quite happy to share any accommodation with Enid. She would never be a close friend, but she had become fond of her.

'Which bed do you want, Enid? I'm not fussy – as long as it's got sheets and a pillow, it will suit me just fine.'

The thought of attending a party added extra enthusiasm to their ablutions and she wished she'd got more than a clean uniform to put on. However, with washed hair and makeup she was a new woman. She had been issued with a torch and a large umbrella.

Nester poked her head outside. 'It's stopped raining; shall we make a run for it?'

Victoria was bubbling with excitement at the thought that although she was unlikely to meet Taylor this evening, she would meet his fellow officers and be able to ask after him. She did not consider for a moment the remote possibility he could have been injured or killed in the battle; God could not be so unfair.

They tumbled into the mess to be greeted by a huge cheer and a round of applause. She cannoned into Nester and Valerie, who had halted abruptly at the unexpected greeting. The group of thirty or so American officers were suddenly milling around them, shaking their hands and greeting them like old friends.

She was handed from person to person, but all the time she was looking over the shoulder of the man who was talking to her, hoping to see a familiar face. He wasn't there. Her heart shrunk and her smile became forced. She desperately wanted to see Taylor, to discover if the attraction she had felt was anything more than a fleeting fancy.

A charming captain was explaining to her what was planned for the evening. 'We have a grand supper laid on for you ladies, and then some of the guys are doing a show, and there'll be dancing. I hope you ladies know how to jitterbug?'

Victoria nodded. 'Yes, we learnt it in Colombo; there were Americans there as well.'

'I guess you know you're the first ladies we've had visit us here. You're sure going to be in demand.'

She smiled and mumbled something polite. She felt a tap on her shoulder. Surely there couldn't be anyone else she had to greet? She spun and found herself in Taylor's arms. In front of everyone he crushed her to his chest and she tilted her head to receive his kiss.

The noise of the room faded and all she could hear was his breathing. His hard mouth covered hers and for a blissful minute she relaxed into his embrace. However, the raucous cheering from the assembled American officers was more than enough to end the kiss.

2

A SECOND CHANCE?

Taylor stepped back but didn't release her hand. 'I sure am glad to see you, Victoria. I hope I haven't offended you.'

'By kissing me? Absolutely not, but before we get too carried away I need to tell you about myself.' He grinned, his dark blue eyes blazed, and he gathered her closer in a proprietorial way. 'That can wait. Tonight I just want to dance with the most beautiful girl in the room and make sure that the other guys know I've already staked my claim.'

This wasn't quite what she wanted to hear, but if she was going to be monopolised it might as well be by someone as attractive as Taylor King. His kiss had confirmed what she already knew, that for the first time in five years she was physically attracted to a man. But she had no intention of being swept away. Perhaps, when she got to know him a little better she might be prepared to sleep with him, but she certainly didn't want to start anything serious.

It would be foolish to become too involved. She was already drowning in lies and if she let Taylor become close she would either have to reveal her secrets, or deceive him as well. They had a week's R & R – time enough for a brief fling before they were both sent back to the front line.

Victoria spent every moment of the party next to Taylor. They hardly had a chance to exchange more than a few words in private, but she was enjoying dancing with him and holding hands, or standing with their arms around each other. The more physical contact they shared the more certain she became that she was more than ready to embark on a short affair. There were prophylactics available to all servicemen to ensure they did not impregnate their partners – or more importantly catch any unpleasant sexually transmitted diseases.

She wanted to leave early and find somewhere they could talk, but it would have seemed discourteous when the Americans had gone to so much trouble. She had been introduced a dozen times as his sweetheart and the more that happened the more concerned she became that he was reading too much into the relationship. Living so close to death as he did, his senses were heightened and he had elevated their meeting into a grand romance. The sooner she explained the better.

A vast quantity of beer and spirits were consumed and by the time the bar was finally closed at midnight, the last record removed from the turntable, she was more than ready to go back with her friends to her own accommodation. Taylor insisted on walking her through the compound.

'Honey, I've got furlough all this next week and I intend to spend every second of it with you. I've arranged for us to borrow a jeep and go into the hills; there's a monastery we can visit if you like.'

'I'd love to; it's so long since I've been inside any kind of religious building. It would be wonderful just to sit in peace. What time are you calling for me?'

Why had she agreed so readily? His enthusiasm was infectious and if she wasn't careful she'd be swept away by the romance and find herself committed, as she had done once before, to a man she knew nothing about.

'Well it's a little after midnight now; how about I come at eight o'clock? I can grab some rations from the canteen and we can get away immediately.'

'On second thoughts, Taylor, I don't think we should go anywhere until we've had a chance to talk.'

'Okay, we won't go to the monastery. I know this swell place not far from here where we can go and talk and not be disturbed.' He gently stroked her face and his touch sent shock waves around her body. 'I know we've only just met, but I knew the moment I saw you on the train that you were going to be someone special. I feel as if I've known you for years.'

'I know what you mean, but let's not rush into anything. You might change your mind after you know a bit more about me.'

He shook his head. 'I don't give a damn about your past; all I'm interested in is your future. Goodnight, sweetheart.'

She was conscious that her friends were watching so turned her face away so his kiss missed her mouth. 'Goodnight, Taylor. I'll see you tomorrow at eight o'clock.'

* * *

All night she tossed and turned; even the comfort of a real bed failed to soothe her. The drumming of the monsoon rain on the tin roof was keeping her awake as much as her anticipation. She got up at dawn, long before the others, glad to have the bathroom to herself. She decided to have a luxurious soak. Taylor had given her a box of rose-scented talcum powder and a bar of sweet-smelling soap to use.

Freshly scrubbed and in her last clean uniform, she was ready to leave when the knock came at precisely eight o'clock. She left a note for her friends telling them where she was going and with whom, and that she would be back before dark. She was the only one of the group not to have consumed vast quantities of alcohol; they would all be suffering this morning from the most horrendous hangovers and would hardly notice her absence.

She grabbed her holdall. This contained a set of clean underwear, a washbag and makeup, just in case they were needed. No sensible woman ever left a base without taking a change of clothes – and she hoped that he didn't get the wrong idea and think she was intending to sleep with him. A warm glow spread from her toes to her crown at the thought of spending the night with Taylor. It was far too long since she had made love, and Henry wouldn't have wanted her to live like a nun indefinitely.

She quickly unlocked the door before he banged more loudly and woke anyone else up. As soon as she stepped outside she was swept off her feet and soundly kissed, much to the delight of a passing group of GIs.

Flustered, she pushed away from him. 'Put me down, Taylor; everyone's looking. We're both officers. We should behave with more decorum.'

'Gee, honey, can't I give my best girl a kiss when I see her?'

She grinned at his exaggerated accent. 'That reminds me, I've been meaning to ask – why don't you sound more American? Sometimes I hardly notice you're not English.'

He smiled. 'That's because I come from Boston, sweetheart. Those of us who live on Beacon Hill behave as though we're British aristocrats.'

'That explains it. I suppose I should have realised, but I know absolutely nothing about America. I imagine that I could pass for an American where you come from.'

He attempted to take her hand but she stepped away, not wishing to be seen to be intimately involved with an American who, to all intents and purposes, she had only just met. They strolled towards the transport area where the borrowed jeep awaited them.

'Are you thinking of emigrating to the grand old US of A?'

She flushed. Where had that come from? He would think she had designs on him. What must he think of a woman who'd only known him five minutes and was already planning to move to Boston?

He seemed amused rather than shocked by her faux pas. 'I guess things are moving a bit fast. Let's forget about the future and concentrate on the here and now. What do you say?'

They had reached the jeep and she tossed her bag behind the front seat and couldn't fail to notice that his was already there. She scrambled in and turned to him, her face serious. 'An excellent idea, Taylor. Let's not turn a physical attraction into something it isn't.'

His smile vanished and for a moment he looked far less affable. Then he shrugged and his charming grin was back. 'There was something you wanted to tell me, Victoria, so we might as well talk here.'

He couldn't have made it clearer. Her frank remark had shocked him and he was no longer sure he wished to go anywhere with her. 'I have been married before, when I was seventeen, but my husband was killed at Dunkirk. I have not looked at another man since. When I met you on the train all those weeks ago, I felt an immediate attraction to you and believe that you felt the same thing.' She swallowed. This wasn't going too well. He was frowning slightly and had shifted away from her.

'I fell in love with Henry instantly, and he with me, but we had a pitifully short time together. I don't regret a minute of it. But I never want to go through what I experienced when I got that telegram. The grief almost killed me. I vowed never to fall in love again until this wretched war's over, and I'm sure the man I love is not likely to be killed.'

His face was transformed and his eyes glittered. 'I understand. But I can't help the way I feel. I'm not going to pressure you into anything, but I want you to know, sweetheart, you're the girl for me. Whatever happens over these next few days I shall come and find you at the end of the war and we can take it from there.'

'Thank you, Taylor. I'm so relieved you understand. Can we just enjoy each other's company and see how it goes?' She looked down, embarrassed for a moment to say what was in her mind, then decided she was being silly. 'I think I shocked you when I talked about the physical attraction. But nowadays a couple could die at any time – so why should they ignore what they feel? In peacetime things were different, but now everyone is living in the present and can do things they wouldn't have dreamt of doing a few years ago.'

His smile was positively wolfish. 'If you're suggesting we drive into the hills for a roll in the hay, honey, I won't say no.'

Hearing it put so plainly made her reconsider. 'Captain King, I was talking generally, not specifically. I have no intention of, as you so crudely put it, "rolling in the hay", with you, today. Now, are we going for a drive, or do you want me to get out of this vehicle?'

He laughed out loud and slammed the gears into place. 'We'll go for a picnic. I've got a hamper in the back, and I promise I'll have you back unmolested by dark. Hang on, honey, I don't want you to fall out.'

The jeep bounced and rattled out of the base and onto what was little more than a dirt track. They had travelled no more than a few hundred yards from the base before the sound of the jungle overwhelmed her. She closed her eyes, drinking in the chittering, squawking and rustling, which took her back to a time before she was an adult.

She had just spent six weeks surrounded by the same noises, but had been far too busy saving lives to pay attention to her surroundings. They hit a pothole and she was flung painfully into the door. Taylor was unrepentant. 'I told you to hold on. I am your superior officer and you should have obeyed my order.'

'You are a captain in the American army not the British, and therefore I am not obligated to obey anything you say.' She gripped the edge of the door and the seat. 'However, if you're going to drive like a maniac, I shall certainly take the proper precautions from now on.'

A further painful twenty minutes passed before he wrenched the wheel to the right and headed for what looked like an impenetrable wall of undergrowth and bushes. They burst through and rocked to a standstill.

'How absolutely beautiful; I would never have known that there was a waterfall hidden behind the bushes. I'm not surprised no one else comes here. Thank you so much for bringing me.'

Not waiting for his assistance, or bothering to struggle with the door catch, she scrambled out and ran across the grass to stare down at the small pool into which the stream tumbled. She had more sense than to attempt to paddle; there would be water snakes and other nasty things lurking in the depths.

'Here, Victoria, I've got a blanket and some deckchairs. Do you want to give me a hand getting them out or are you going to stand there gazing at the vista?' He had thought of everything, including a battered card table on which to put the picnic hamper. 'I've got soda and beer – you can have whichever you want.'

'Beer, please. What's in this? I didn't have time for breakfast and I'm starving.' She patted the wicker top of the basket.

'I'm in the dark; I just asked for a picnic. Could be anything. Shall we have a look?' With great ceremony he unbuckled the leather straps and threw back the lid. 'Gee, not quite what I expected, but we certainly won't go hungry.' He frowned and poked about. 'I hope you don't mind eating native food.'

She felt a flicker of unease, which made her wonder if Taylor wasn't the man she thought he was. After all, it wasn't so long ago that black people were actually real slaves in America. 'I love Indian food, and I actually prefer not to eat meat if possible.' The food wasn't wrapped in banana leaves but neatly contained in spotless mess tins. It tasted delicious and had definitely been prepared by an Indian chef.

Taylor tucked in with equal enthusiasm. Over lunch they got to know each other better; it was hard to be formal when you were eating. There was still quite a lot left over by the time they were both full. 'I think I'll tip this into the undergrowth before we leave – I'm sure the monkeys will enjoy finishing it up for us. I'm going to have a mango; do you want to share with me?'

'Hang on a minute, honey, you'll need this before you start.' With a flourish he produced a crisply ironed khaki handkerchief and solemnly tucked it into the neck of her shirt. 'I promise not to watch whilst you get messy.'

Whilst she devoured the sweet, succulent fruit there was the distinctive click of a lighter as he lit a cigarette. She would have preferred it if he was smoking a beedi; the smell of the local cigarettes was non-invasive and more reminiscent of a bonfire than tobacco.

Strange that she hadn't tasted or smelled tobacco on him when he'd kissed her. She glanced at him and smiled. He wasn't really smoking; he was just taking an occasional pull and then blowing smoke into the gathering cloud of insects attracted by the scent of her mango.

She quickly wiped the residue from her face and threw the half-eaten fruit down the slope towards the waterfall. 'I'm done, thanks. The picnic was delicious.

We seem to be attracting an unwelcome audience. Shall I throw away the leftovers whilst you pack everything away?'

'Do that. Cigarette smoke will only keep them away for so long – then we'll be enveloped in the bloody things.'

In less than five minutes they were ready to leave. Taylor reversed the jeep and then scrambled out to rearrange the branches so that no one else would visit his secret place. Soon they were bumping back down the hill and Victoria regretted that she had eaten so much as her lunch frequently threatened to return unexpectedly.

Fortunately, the journey was quicker downhill, and in less than an hour Taylor drove through the camp gates and parked the jeep alongside several others. 'There's a film being shown this afternoon. It's called *Holiday Inn* and has a couple of guys called Bing Crosby and Fred Astaire in it. I reckon it's a musical. Shall we go and see it?'

He sounded so disgusted at the thought she was tempted to refuse but she could count the times she had seen a moving picture on one hand. 'I should absolutely love to – thank you so much for offering.'

'There was a decent western on last week but we have to see whatever we get.'

'Any film is a good film as far as I'm concerned. Do I have time to use the restroom?'

'Why don't you go back to your quarters and freshen up? I'll meet you here in fifteen minutes and we can grab a coffee before it starts.'

3

SECOND THOUGHTS

After the film the audience remained in a celebratory mood and Victoria and Taylor joined in the stampede to the officers' mess. Although they did not spend every minute together she was always aware he was in the room somewhere. He was universally charming and by the end of the evening she was falling under his spell, despite her determination to remain at a distance. She hoped it was the excess of alcohol she had consumed that was making her think differently about him.

He didn't attempt to kiss her goodnight and she was disappointed. He said he would look her up the next day and then, with a casual wave, walked off with his friends.

Enid linked arms with her, more to hold herself upright than anything else. 'Golly, Victoria, how did you manage to pull the best-looking man on the base?'

'Thanks very much – are you implying that I'm not good enough for him?' Her mock severity was somewhat spoilt as they both stumbled noisily into the side of a building.

Her friend giggled. 'No, of course not. But word has it Captain King hasn't so much as looked at another woman since he arrived on the base.'

'He was pining for me; don't forget we met weeks ago. I think he's rather gorgeous but I'm trying not to fall for him. I don't want the complication of forming a relationship with an American.'

'Don't be daft, he doesn't want to marry you; he's got other things on his mind. You should have seen the way he was looking at you – I'm surprised you didn't burst into flames.'

The door to their accommodation was open, which was fortunate as she didn't think she could have negotiated a closed door in her inebriated state. Giggling and staggering, she fumbled and banged her way to the bedroom.

'Victoria, I've got some "you know whats" if you

need them. Betty gave some to me,' Enid called sleepily.

'No thank you, I'm not that sort of a girl.'

There was an explosion of laughter from the other side of the partition wall. 'Well I am, so if you don't want him, send him in my direction,' Nester called loudly.

* * *

Victoria woke with a mouth like a parrot cage and a pounding headache. She was a nurse, for God's sake, she should have known better than to have drunk so much and then not rehydrated before she went to bed. Feeling decidedly grumpy she rolled out and was relieved to find the bathroom vacant. After a hot shower she felt a bit better but still not ready to face the world.

Why was it so quiet? She'd been so desperate to get to the bathroom she hadn't stopped to see if Enid was still asleep. She wrapped herself in a towel, grabbed her washbag and rushed back to her room to find it empty. There was a note propped up on the dressing table. Good grief – it was almost midday – everyone had gone out and left her to sleep.

Taylor would think she had stood him up. Feverishly she scrambled into her freshly laundered uniform, ran a comb through her hair and shot out into the central recreation area. She almost fell over her feet when she saw the room was occupied.

'Hi there, hope you don't mind my waiting in here for you, honey.' Taylor rose smoothly to his feet and moved slowly towards her.

'I am so sorry. Someone should have woken me up. I can't remember when I last slept for so long.'

'You drank rather a lot last night; I don't suppose you're used to it. I reckon you could do with a strong black coffee.'

'That would be wonderful. What I really need to do is drink a pint of water and take a couple of aspirin. I'll be tickety-boo after that.'

'How do you feel about visiting that monastery today?' There was something about the way he said it, the way he was looking at her so intently, that made her realise this was a pivotal point in their burgeoning relationship. If she agreed to accompany him it was tantamount to saying she wanted to move things on to a more intimate level. A rush of heat scalded her cheeks at the thought of making love to him.

'If you don't mind waiting for a few minutes longer I'll grab my overnight bag.'

There – she'd committed herself. Today she was

she going to sleep with another man, and one that wasn't her husband. What if she changed her mind once they were there? Would he respect her wishes? She didn't think he was the sort of man who would force his attentions on her, but his charming exterior might be a facade.

She grabbed her bag but almost changed her mind when she stepped out into the sunshine and saw him lounging against the wall. Was she the sort of woman who could have a physical affair without her emotions becoming entangled as well?

He took her bag from her hand and threw his other arm around her shoulders. There was no going back now; anyone seeing them together would know they were already an item. They headed for the parking lot and he guided her towards a jeep.

'Climb in, honey. It's a long drive and we don't want to be out in the dark.'

She did as he asked and he threw the vehicle into gear and they shot out of the camp gates. He saluted in his sloppy American way and the GI on duty responded.

His comment about them arriving before dark meant she would have no option but to stay overnight, even if she did change her mind about sleeping with him. Taylor had made it quite plain that he wanted her; was she allowing herself to be taken advantage of? After all, he'd not actually said anything about them having a future together. Maybe he just wanted to sleep with her, like all the rest of the men she'd met since she joined up.

She was being ridiculous – hadn't it been she who had suggested that sleeping with a man without benefit of clergy was perfectly acceptable in wartime? Then the thought that she might appear lacking in morals if she gave in so easily made her decide she wouldn't sleep with him. She would sleep *beside* him, but that was all. If he wanted to become intimate then he would just have to wait until they were married like Henry had.

Where had that come from? How could she be thinking about marrying Taylor after all her protestations to the contrary? She risked a surreptitious glance in his direction, but he was concentrating on the lethal track and appeared unaware of her scrutiny. She jammed herself into the corner so she could grip the door and the back of the seat. He really was a most attractive man – but was this enough on which to base the rest of her life?

She knew he was from Boston, was kind, thoughtful and intelligent, but she didn't want to get involved with someone she couldn't be totally honest with. From his slightly derogatory comment about native food she rather feared his reaction to her mixed ancestry would not be favourable. No – she was going to enjoy spending twenty-four hours in his company, but was certainly not going to sleep with him or consider him as a suitable life partner.

The journey through the overgrown tracks led slowly and steadily up a mountainside. The air was becoming thinner, and colder, and she was glad she had her greatcoat with her.

Conversation over the noise of the engine was impossible but they exchanged smiles and shouted the odd remark as they were flung from side to side each time a wheel dropped into a hole or bounced over a stone.

After a couple of hours they came to clearing and Taylor stopped, slamming the brakes on.

'Shall we take a break for a while? I have so much to say to you and now we're stationary we can talk.'

'Yes, good idea, Taylor. I think we need to get something straight between us before we carry on. The fact that we are staying somewhere together overnight doesn't mean that I intend to sleep with you.'

'I didn't think it did – you're not that kind of girl. I've got my things in the back for exactly the same reason you have. I never travel without them. I've also got rations, water, a first-aid kit, spare gas, planks, a foot pump, a spade and a few other things besides. I don't travel anywhere without them either.'

'Thank you, I'm relieved we've got that clear. I think I might have misled you yesterday. I know there's a war on, and lots of young women sleep around, but it doesn't mean I have to sacrifice my principles even if other people do.' As soon as she'd spoken she knew she'd sounded prudish. After all she wasn't a shy young virgin; she'd been married before, knew everything about bedroom matters.

He reached over, taking her hands in his. She gazed down at his long, lean fingers, so different from Henry's, but they still had the strength to hold and protect her should she need it. 'Listen to me, honey, there's nothing I'd like better than to make love to you, but I know the score and don't expect you to compromise in order to indulge me. Let's forget about it, shall we? Let's enjoy the rest of the trip. It's just magic being with you – I don't need anything else.'

The monastery was tucked away on a stony plateau. The ancient building was surrounded by lush vegetation with orchids growing in the overhanging branches and a clear stream gurgling down the rocks into a pool filled with crystal-clear water.

'This is an incredible place, so peaceful and spiritual, but it seems to be deserted. Where are all the monks?'

'This part of the front has been occupied by the Japanese a couple of times. We've driven them back now – they're several miles away – but the monks left believing they would be safer further behind the Indian line.'

'That's a pity, but at least we can go and have a look round.'

She didn't wait for him to help her down; those days had long gone. In the army you were expected to look after yourself whatever gender you were. The main room of the low stone building was cool and dry; no furniture, just stones where the monks must have sat telling their prayer beads. She felt the peace of the building calm her jangled nerves and sat down on one of the stones, bowing her head in prayer.

She didn't know how long she'd been sitting there, but was suddenly aware she was alone. Surely he'd not given up and gone away? She jumped to her feet and looked around. Yes, she was by herself. She didn't like to call out even though the monastery was abandoned; it wasn't the sort of place you shouted. She ran outside into the sunshine and was relieved to see the jeep was parked where they'd left it. Her heart settled to a more regular beat and she walked over, thinking she might toot the horn to attract his attention.

She climbed on the step and looked inside. Their overnight bags and several of the other boxes had vanished from behind the seats so he must be setting up camp somewhere. She doubted she would have the strength of character not to respond to him if he tried to seduce her.

She jumped down and went to look for him. There was still time to get back to camp if they left straightaway. She was quite happy to go without supper if it meant she didn't have to spend the night alone with him.

It wasn't that she didn't trust him; she didn't trust herself. Every time he kissed her or when he held her hand, she felt a surge of desire that almost overwhelmed her. She'd never felt this way with Henry; it had taken time to become accustomed to their intimacy. She'd had to learn to relax and not be embarrassed by her body or his.

She only had to be within arm's reach of Taylor and her pulse raced. It wouldn't take much for her to agree to sleep with him. Would it be so bad if she did? After all they could both be killed tomorrow – hadn't she said war concentrated the mind on what was important?

Perhaps she was being overcautious. Angela, and possibly one or two of the other girls, was more than ready to sleep with any man who took her fancy. Somehow nobody seemed to think the worse of them; maybe by making love to a soldier about to go into battle they were doing their bit for the war effort.

She giggled at the absurdity of the analogy. Good God, whatever would Marion and Arthur – Henry's parents – think? Instantly she sobered. She tried not to think of England because of her daughter, Amelia, who would be approaching her fifth birthday soon, and must wonder why her mother had abandoned her. Her arms ached with emptiness and she made her decision. She went in search of Taylor. There must be dormitories, a refectory, ablutions and so on somewhere. The monks were men after all and had bodily functions like other mortals.

'Taylor, Taylor, can you hear me? Where are you?'

She heard him calling, his voice echoing strangely in the empty building. 'I'm getting us something to eat, sweetheart. I've found the kitchen – it's pretty basic but it'll do.'

By following his voice, she found him in a sunny room at the rear of the building stoking a wood-burning stove. He smiled and her insides melted with lust. Without hesitation, she threw herself into his arms. Her kiss told him everything he needed to know.

To her astonishment it was he who broke the embrace, gently removing her arms from around his neck and stepping away. 'I know just how you feel, hon, but you don't have to do this, not for me. I don't want to rush things either. I think, no dammit, I know you're the one – you're the woman I've been waiting for all this time.'

'That's not very long, Taylor. How old are you? You can't be much older than I am.'

'I'm twenty-five, and you are?'

'I'm twenty-three. I was married at seventeen and widowed two years later.' She was about to blurt out that she had a child in Britain, but the moment passed.

'So, you're a woman of experience? Are you going to teach me how things are done?' His slow smile sent waves of heat around her body. His strange blue-grey eyes glittered with an intensity she recognised. Now was the time to tell him she'd changed her mind, that she wanted to consummate their relationship. But she held back. She would regret it if she did. She needed to spend more time with him, get to know him a little better before she shared her body with him.

Instead they shared a pleasant meal of rehydrated

rations heated up over the wood-burning stove, washed down with stewed tea.

'I thought Americans preferred coffee?'

'I do, as a rule, but over here the tea tastes different, and as there is so little coffee available, I've learnt to adjust.'

They decided to stay the night after all, but sleep in separate dormitories. These all had stone shelves that they could put their bedrolls on and sleep relatively comfortably.

'If we do stay, Taylor, everyone will assume we're sleeping together. This will make things awkward for both of us.'

'I can think of one way that it wouldn't: if you agree to marry me.' He slipped the words into the conversation so casually for a moment the meaning didn't register. Her head shot round.

'Taylor King, did you just ask me to marry you?'

'I sure did, ma'am, what do you say?'

'You don't have to marry me to get me into bed, you know. I could easily be persuaded without that. I find you... well, I find you quite attractive, if you must know.'

His rich laughter filled the room. 'Quite attractive? Why, that makes me feel just great. I can't wait to tell my buddies that the woman I just asked to marry me finds me *quite attractive*.'

She blushed at his teasing tone. 'Well, you know we British are the masters of understatement. Actually, I find you irresistible, but I can hardly say that, can I?'

His eyes were laughing, but she detected a certain hesitancy in his manner as he moved closer, stroking her hair away from her face with gentle fingers. 'You haven't answered my question, Victoria? Will you marry me? I know we've only just met, but I've never been surer of anything in my whole life.'

She had intended to say no, but she spoke without thought. 'Yes, yes – I will. I think I also knew the moment you spoke to me on the train that I'd met my second husband.' She leant forward to receive his kiss and it was light, his lips merely brushing hers, no sign of the passion she'd felt vibrating between them.

'I think we'd better go back to camp and share the good news with everyone. I want to marry you, I love you, but I don't want to sleep with you until our wedding night,' she said.

'Sure thing – if that's the way you want it, it's okay by me. You grab the gear – I spread it out in the dormitories earlier – whilst I put this fire out. We can be away in no time.' He went to the window and peered out. 'Looks okay out there, no sign of black clouds; if we're lucky we'll get back before the rains start again.'

It was strange packing up their things, feeling ownership for his belongings as well as hers. She was engaged to a man she'd known for barely forty-eight hours. Well, that wasn't quite true as she'd met him in India more than two months ago, if only for half an hour.

She prayed this second relationship would last longer than the first. Thinking about Henry, and how short a time they'd had together, made her think about the immediate future. A handful of pencils spilled onto the rear seat. Puzzled she unbuckled his bag to put them back. Her eyes were drawn to an artist pad.

'Taylor, you didn't say you were an artist.'

He was stowing things under the seat and buckling the straps on the lockers and straightened. 'Have a look. It's my passion. Keeps me sane. I was sketching whilst you were meditating.'

She pulled out the pad and flipped it open. Her breath caught in her throat. 'These are wonderful.' She paused at the first of several sketches of herself. 'These are so good, rather flattering, but lovely.'

He grinned. 'They don't do you justice, honey. You're the most beautiful woman I've ever seen.' He returned to his task and her blush faded.

'Taylor, have you thought how long we should be engaged before we marry?'

He glanced over his shoulder. 'If you want me to, honey, I can speak to my CO and the padre. I reckon we could be married by the end of the week.' He turned back, busying himself in the rear of the vehicle, giving her time to make her decision.

'Yes, if we want to get married before the end of the war, it will have to be now. The British Army is very sticky about such things. They won't want to lose me and rarely agree to marriages where both members are serving. However, at the moment my CO is Valerie, and she might be a bit straitlaced, but she's a romantic at heart. I'm sure she'll agree. What about your commanding officer?'

He straightened and reaching out, lifted her easily from her feet until she was straddling him. 'We Yanks have a more relaxed attitude about getting hitched. Our CO is a strict Episcopalian – he'd rather we married than burn in sin.'

She relaxed against him, loving the feel of his heart beating heavily against hers. 'Burning in sin sounds very attractive. I'm not sure I wouldn't prefer it to the holy state of matrimony.'

His arms tightened and even through the double

thickness of their clothes she felt the hardness in his groin.

'Then, if we're going to do this properly, the sooner we get back to camp and get things organised the better. If you remember, the last time I got leave two months ago, I was recalled after twenty-four hours.'

'So was I and we were forced to miss our date in Madras. You're right. Let's get moving. With luck the major will be in the mess and I can speak to her tonight.'

He drove like a madman, allowing Victoria no room for second thoughts as she was too worried about plunging off the path to her death.

4

MORE LIES

The jeep raced into the base just as the clouds rolled in. The two GIs guarding at the gate grinned and waved them through; here no one bothered to salute. Victoria found this lack of protocol unnerving as she'd become accustomed to the rules and regulations that glued the British Army together. The discipline and toughness of the British Forces had kept the Germans at bay for so long.

She wasn't sure about the Yanks. They seemed so slack, slouching around in unkempt uniforms waving rather than saluting. Even when they did salute it was in a haphazard kind of way. However, whatever they lacked in appearance and discipline they more than made up for with their superior equipment and money. Without the Americans on their side she doubted Britain would still be a free country.

'Listen, hon, will you speak to your CO this afternoon? I'll find my major. We should be able to arrange things for tomorrow. If we do, that will give us thirty-six hours for our honeymoon.'

'Won't we have to have a special licence or something?'

'No, there's a war on; the authorities know time's short. When guys get a twenty-four pass they can be married and back on duty before you know it.'

'You're right, I'd forgotten. It's so long since I was in England I'd no idea how things had changed, and to tell the truth, I don't think anyone I've been working with has actually got married. We've not been in any one place long enough to get to know...' Her voice faltered. Taylor and she had known each other for less than four days and they were getting married. Although, if you counted the intervening weeks since they had first met on the train, they had known each other for over two months.

Their arrival had been noticed by Enid who was returning with Angela and Betty from the officers' mess. Victoria waved. 'I'll see you later in the bar. I'm going to try and find Valerie and get her permission. I'll bring my birth certificate and so on with me this evening.'

She jumped down and she was about to run over to join her friends when he called her back. 'Hang on a minute, sweetheart, what about your gear?'

In her hurry to share her news she'd forgotten that her holdall, bedroll and haversack were still in the locker behind the seat. Her friends were waiting, but didn't approach. 'You go on, honey; I'll drop your things off at your accommodation.'

She smiled at him and saw his jaw tighten. His eyes glittered, the blue-grey becoming almost black. Laughing at his reaction, she ran across the concrete to join the three young women standing impatiently outside the mess. As she got there the first heavy splashes of rain began to drum on the tin roof.

'Come on, girls, we'll have to run for it if we don't want to get drenched again.' Angela led the way along the paths and they threw themselves into their temporary home.

'I'm soaked to my knickers,' Victoria announced solemnly. 'I shall have to wear my dressing gown; my spare things are still in the back of the jeep.'

'Your clean laundry is back; there's an efficient

system here. I stowed it in your locker, so you've got dry stuff to put on,' Enid told her with a grin.

Angela wrung out her hair. 'One good thing about this rain: it makes your hair really soft.'

'Victoria, we didn't expect you back tonight. Has something happened? Did you and your handsome captain fall out?' Betty asked, obviously hoping this was the case.

She looked from one to the other, unsure how they would take her astonishing news. 'Actually, something did happen. Taylor asked me to marry him and I said yes. We've returned to try and get it arranged for tomorrow. If we don't, we might have to wait until the end of the war, and God knows how long that might be.'

Enid screamed. 'I knew it! I said to the others you and Taylor were made for each other. He's absolutely gorgeous – I don't blame you for grabbing him whilst you can. If I was in your shoes I'd do the same.'

The other two added their congratulations and none of them suggested she was foolhardy, or that she should wait. There was a glow inside her that even the torrential rain couldn't extinguish.

The engagement was another excuse for a riotous party in the officers' mess. The documents necessary for their marriage had been produced on both sides, along with permission from Taylor's major and Valerie.

The padre was delighted to have something other than burials to perform.

The ceremony was set for ten o'clock the following morning, which would allow them plenty of time to drive back to the monastery where they intended to spend the remaining two days of their leave. Everyone seemed pleased for them. She was kissed and hugged by dozens of Taylor's friends and they all told her that he was a great guy, that she'd got one of the best, and she believed them.

At ten o'clock precisely they stood in the chapel dressed in their normal uniforms and said their vows. Taylor had found a slim gold band from somewhere to slip on her finger, promising he would get her something better after the war. She didn't care – her left hand had felt naked since she had removed Henry's ring.

She drove away from the base less than twenty-four hours since she'd returned, but now she was a different person; she was Mrs Taylor King. They rattled and bumped their way back to the monastery and this time the jeep was loaded with bedding, rations, beer, and other things that Taylor's buddies had thought essential for his honeymoon.

She closed her eyes and allowed her mind to drift over the incredible events of the past few days. She was now enmeshed in a third set of lies. In order to get married she had had to produce the bogus birth certificate her father had had forged so long ago. On it she had a set of mythical parents who had lived in Kent – another lot of imaginary relatives and places to remember.

When she was Henry's wife she'd had to talk about parents who had been born in India and died; now she had to remember that her parents had been English and had lived in Kent until their demise. She didn't even know where Kent was. How could she possibly answer any questions?

Scalding tears squeezed out and a wave of despair almost crushed her happiness. Would she have to spend the rest of her life living under a shadow? Would there ever be a time when the people she loved would know who she really was? Or would she go to her grave pretending to be someone she wasn't?

Victoria turned her face away from Taylor, not wishing him to see her tears and think she was regretting their impulsive marriage. She was too late; his hand left the wheel and gripped her knee.

'What's wrong? Not having second thoughts already? Everything will be fine. We've made the right decision, honey; we were meant to be together. I promise you, after tonight, you'll not have any regrets.'

She wiped her eyes on the back of her hand but didn't look round. She couldn't think of anything to say. His words were meant to reassure her, but had done the reverse. Did he think sex was her motivation? Did he honestly believe by making love to her, he could put things right? She stared at the man beside her. Had he asked her to become his wife because they loved each other or because he lusted after her and could get her no other way?

He swore, using words that made her ears burn. Then slamming on the brakes, he brought the jeep skidding to a halt, almost pitching her over the side.

'For God's sake, Victoria, don't look like that. I shouldn't have pushed you into this; it was too soon. You Brits need time to think. Americans are impulsive – react first, think about it afterwards.' He reached out and almost dragged her across the seat, banging her hip painfully on the gearstick as he pulled her onto his lap. Cradling her head in one hand, he put his other around her waist and stared down at her, his eyes blazing with love.

With shaking fingers she stretched out to trace the

outline of his face, feeling the rasp of bristles under her fingertips, the slight indentation in the end of his chin, then running her hand up to the crinkles on either side of his eyes. Her fingers tangled in his short brown hair, pulling his face down to meet her lips.

They kissed with a desperation, a passion they had not shown before. In that one kiss she learnt how much he loved her and she told him she returned his love.

'Christ! I want you so much, but I'm not going to make love to you for the first time in the front seat of a jeep.' He firmly removed her hands and lifted her back across the vehicle, then switching the engine back on he engaged the gears and shot off.

She watched him concentrating on his driving, seeing his knuckles were white where he gripped the steering wheel, his blue-grey eyes fixed ahead. She knew exactly how he felt; she was burning up inside. She'd never felt this way with Henry, never felt so desperate to be in bed with him she would let nothing stand in her way. Her eyes widened. She knew now why people said such stupid things, why people died for it, killed for it – at that moment if someone tried to take her away from Taylor she would fight to the death to stay by his side.

The wild drive was long enough for them both to

have recovered their senses and bring their passion under control. They unloaded the jeep together, carefully avoiding even the most accidental brush of fingers, knowing the slightest touch would ignite the conflagration. Like dancers they tiptoed around each other, smiling politely, speaking inanities instead of conversation.

This continued until everything had been placed where it should be. Taylor mumbled something about sorting out the latrine and left her to find somewhere to make up their bed. She checked what she had been given. There were six double blankets that Taylor had borrowed from someone in the quartermaster's store, their bedrolls and a mysterious brown paper parcel tied up with white, hairy string.

The single bunks the monks had used weren't suitable. The only room with enough space to make up a double bed was in what had been the monk's refectory. This had a large open fireplace, which meant they could keep warm when the rain came. She smiled wryly. She doubted that heat from an external source was going to be necessary.

Dropping to her knees she arranged the six blankets as a mattress then spread out the two sleeping bags on top. She found a knife in her haversack and cut the string on the parcel. Inside were a pair of double sheets. She felt her eyes fill at the thoughtfulness of her husband. What other man would understand how important having real bed linen would be to her?

She stood up, certain there was nothing else she could do to make their bed more comfortable. She wasn't sure what she should do. Should she undress and wait for him to come to her? Or would he expect her to go to the kitchen and start preparing a meal? She stepped away from the bed, deciding it might be premature to remove her clothes; after all it was barely mid-afternoon.

When she turned to leave she heard him approaching at a run. Taylor arrived in the doorway. His eyes looked straight over her shoulder and then back to her.

Seeing her answer, he was beside her in two strides, pressing her against his chest, kissing her with such fervour her knees buckled. She couldn't remember taking her clothes off but somehow they were naked between the sheets and making wonderful, joyous, uninhibited love.

Hours later Taylor propped himself up on one elbow, his other arm resting possessively on her naked breast. 'Darling, I'm starving. How about you?'

She barely had the energy to answer. 'If you're prepared to make something, I think I can eat. I could do with a drink, and I must use the facilities.'

Taylor jumped to his feet, unashamedly naked, and pulled her up beside him. For a moment she was embarrassed, wanting to cover herself with something.

He kissed her gently. 'We're married, honey; there's no need to be shy with me. I'm afraid the facilities are a bit basic, but at least I've rigged something up inside.'

She stepped off the makeshift bed and the cold stone floor sent an icy shock wave up through the soles of her feet. 'Good God! I'm not traipsing around like this – it's far too cold.' She looked around for something to put on and the first item she found was Taylor's shirt. She shrugged it on. It came down to just below her bottom and the sleeves fell over the end of her hands.

'You look like an orphan in that. Here, honey, hold out your arms and I'll roll the sleeves up for you.'

Next, she pulled on her socks and reluctantly he agreed that it was far too cold to remain unclothed and pulled on his trousers.

* * *

They spent the next thirty-six hours in bed, making love, eating, watching the fire burn in the grate, listening to the rain pounding on the roof, both deliriously happy. She forgot about the lies she'd had to tell him, just revelled in being held and made love to by a man she loved in return. He also found time to draw. Although they hadn't discussed it, she believed he was extremely talented, might even be able to make his living from his work if he wished to.

When it was time to leave they were so close they no longer needed to talk – a smile, a touch, was enough. Their marriage hadn't been a mistake. Whatever happened in the future, what she felt for her new husband was as powerful as the love she'd had for Henry; in fact stronger, because it was the love of a mature woman not a shy young girl.

When they were ready to drive away the monastery was as pristine as when they'd arrived. She stood for a few minutes holding his hand, looking around, imprinting the place on her memory, glad they had his sketches to remind them of this magical place.

'I don't know when we'll be together again, sweetheart, but I promise you if I can get a pass, I'll come and find you. Even if we only spend ten minutes together, I'll still come.'

'I shall be too busy once the field hospital is up and running to get any time off. Last time it was only for two months and then we packed up and I got leave. God willing it will be the same again.'

'I should have asked before, do you know when you had your last monthly? What's the chance of you being pregnant?'

She grinned. 'Every chance, I should think, after the number of times we've made love.'

'Well, if you discover you are, you'll have to leave the service. Go back to the camp and wait for me there. If you send me a message it'll reach me eventually.'

The thought that she might be pregnant hadn't occurred to her until he'd mentioned it. A shiver of anticipation rippled down her spine. Would having another baby make the loss of Amelia less painful or more difficult? She stiffened. If she was pregnant and wished to be discharged then an MO would have to examine her. He would know immediately she had been pregnant before. However confidential medical records were, this information would be seen by others, and someone might tell Taylor.

If she was pregnant she would keep the information to herself until she was so far along she would have no need to see a doctor to have it confirmed. Last time she had been horribly sick, but she hadn't looked pregnant until she was five months. She prayed if she was pregnant this time she would be spared the morning sickness. It would be impossible to hide her condition living with a group of nurses.

'I can't remember the last time I had the curse, Taylor; in fact, since I've been out here I don't think I've had it very often. I'm sure everything will be fine; you mustn't worry. If there's the slightest chance I'm expecting a baby I'll let you know at once.'

'Would you mind if you were? I must say I would be delighted if you were no longer working on the front line, but I'd like to have some time alone with you before having to share you with a baby.'

She stepped in close, pulling his head down. 'Whatever happens, I promise you will always come first with me. I shall always love you, however many children we may have in the future. We'll share them; they'll never come between us.'

Her answer appeared to satisfy him and his face cleared. 'Come on, honey, we'd better get a move on. I have to report at eighteen hundred hours.'

Back at base most people were preparing to move out. Victoria scrambled out of the jeep and into Taylor's waiting arms. 'Take care of yourself, sweetheart. I've got more reason to stay alive now I have you waiting for me.' He kissed her once and they embraced briefly. She smiled, unable to answer, and stepped away. Then she turned and ran to join the others, hoping their cheerful chatter would distract her from the agony of parting for the second time from a husband she loved beyond words.

PART II

BOSTON, USA, 1944–46

5

AN AMERICAN NOW?

Victoria hadn't been surprised to discover she was pregnant after their honeymoon; after all she had fallen with Amelia as quickly. This second child could never replace the daughter she'd left behind, but he or she would help repair the hole in her heart. She wasn't plagued with appalling morning sickness; maybe it was because she was too busy saving lives in the jungle to worry about her own health. She had been sick a couple of times but not enough to arouse suspicion and had been able to continue working, her secret undetected, until the field hospital was no longer needed and she returned with her fellow nurses to an English base. Here she'd then admitted her condition to Valerie.

By this time she was four months and there was no need for more than a cursory examination by the chief medical officer. She had sent a message to Taylor's unit and within three days received a reply. He managed to arrange for her to fly to America on a military plane. She was privileged to be allowed on board one of these, as they were usually reserved exclusively for members of the American Forces and she was neither American, nor war service personnel.

He couldn't get away himself – whatever his unit was involved in hadn't finished – but he'd made arrangements for her to fly out from Calcutta. All she had to do was present herself at the American airbase when she was ready to leave. A seat would be found for her on the next available flight.

Victoria had been sorry to say goodbye to the women she'd been working with, but she wasn't sorry to be pregnant. Ever since she'd known she'd been bubbling with excitement. As she was no longer a Queen Alexandra's member she would have no further use for her equipment. She'd left it to be distributed amongst her friends, only taking her holdall and a change of clothes. She didn't actually have a time or date for her departure, had been merely told to report and the rest could be arranged for her.

This suited her perfectly. She could now spend some time contacting her parents and letting them know she was leaving for America and that she was pregnant. Her parents had made the arduous journey across the width of India to spend a final few days with her and she knew whatever happened she would always have their support.

Her father was no longer planning to leave India. He had been invited to stand for parliament and was proud to accept. He was a new breed of Indian Brahmin. A well-bred, well-educated man, who had put his past behind and embraced the thought of republicanism and democracy wholeheartedly.

As instructed, she reported to the airbase and handed over her chit. A harassed GI examined it. 'Okay, ma'am, if you wait just there, I'll see what I can do. I think there could be a seat on the next bus out of here but it won't be comfortable.'

If he was expecting her to complain he was going to be unlucky. 'Thank you, I have just spent the past six months nursing in the jungle so anything that is dry and warm will be a luxury to me.'

He grinned, not at all put out by her reprimand. 'That's swell, ma'am – we sure do appreciate all the work you've been doing to save our boys.'

She found herself a chair in the corner of the chaotic office and was quite happy to wait. She was not looking forward to flying across the world in a military plane as she suffered horribly from airsickness. She ate nothing and drank sparingly – the less she had in her stomach the better.

Eventually she was called over and pointed towards an enormous Douglas C-54 Sky Master at the far end of the strip that was to be her transport to America. 'Have a good flight, ma'am, but you'd better hurry as they'll be ready to leave in five minutes.'

She might be halfway through her pregnancy but she could still run if she had to. She arrived at the rudimentary steps just as the engines fired. She scrambled in and the door was slammed behind her. This time she'd had the sense to bring a large quantity of newspaper and paper bags.

'There's a seat forward, behind the pilot, ma'am, not great but I guess it's better than sitting on the floor.' The young airman didn't offer to carry her luggage, just pointed and she followed his gesture. She had barely settled herself when the plane rolled forward and sped down the runway.

The long, tedious flight gave her ample time to think about the past hectic few weeks. As she shook and jerked unpleasantly in the small seat she smiled.

Her father might be a republican now, but her mother had told her he still had a safe full of precious stones and easily portable assets. He had prepared himself for whatever eventuality might transpire. He could remain in India and become a successful politician, leading his country forward into a bright new future, or slip away quietly to a new life in England. Whatever happened he'd made quite certain his wealth was secure.

She was grateful for the thick coat and flying helmet she'd been loaned for the journey. Without them she would have frozen. The transatlantic flight was nothing like the one she'd taken from India to England. That time she had travelled in luxury, her every whim catered for, this time she was merely an inconvenience. Pregnant women were treated with respect by the Americans. They appeared to honour their womenfolk and in spite of the primitive conditions, and the fact that she was a nuisance on an all-male flight, they had done their best to make her feel at home.

Thank God, this time she hadn't needed the bags so thoughtfully provided and had been able to surreptitiously hide the newspapers under the seat. What nausea she'd experienced in the early months of her pregnancy had now gone as she entered the middle of her second trimester. Knowing so much more about the medical side of things meant she could check her own progress, know that her pregnancy was progressing well. The baby she was carrying was the correct size. The fact that she could already feel him kicking was another good sign.

She had already decided this time she was having a boy. No reason, apart from she'd felt so much better, and was much bigger than she had been at this stage with Amelia. Of course, some of that was due to it being a second pregnancy – the muscles were already in tune with her body – but she had guessed correctly about Amelia being a girl, so assumed she was correct this time.

As the plane dropped like a stone, she gripped the sides of her seat and prayed. This was an air pocket, nothing to worry about, but she hated the sensation. She didn't think she'd ever really enjoy flying; she much preferred to travel by train or ship.

The plane landed once to refuel and pick up more packages and a few dozen GIs returning for home leave. Most of them were too exhausted to do more than nod in her direction. They didn't have the luxury of seats; they stretched out in whatever space they could find, rolled up in their thick coats, their heads on their packs, and slept throughout the journey.

The pilot turned around, making a thumbs up, then pointed downwards. She nodded and smiled. They were coming in to land; she would soon have her first contact with her new country. Taylor had told her that by her marriage she had become an American, with all the rights under their constitution that he had. Their child would be an American too. How complicated everything was. What was she? An Anglo-Indian daughter, an English widow, or an American wife?

How did the men spreadeagled on the floor manage to stay in one place? As the plane screamed towards the ground through the high cloud they ought to be sliding about. She braced herself for a killing impact. She could never quite believe she would arrive back on the ground in one piece.

The pilot, his navigator and co-pilot were laughing about something; she could hear it even above the howl of the engines. Her tension dissipated a little. If they weren't worried then why should she be? After all they were supposed to be the experts. Her feet brushed against the solid pack of the parachute she'd been issued with when she'd got on. Thank God she hadn't had to don it; the thought of jumping out of a plane into nothingness was too awful to contemplate.

The buffeting and howling lessened and there

were the sound of the wheels going down. A few moments later the ground rushed up to meet them. The plane bounced a couple of times then settled smoothly and the pilot threw the engines into reverse, or whatever it was he did, and applied the brakes. She prayed the runway was long enough for this giant metal machine to stop safely.

She opened her eyes as everything became still. 'Here we are, ma'am, safe and sound. Is someone meeting you?' The far too young pilot stood in front of her.

'Not as far as I know; I couldn't tell my in-laws when or where I would be arriving so they aren't in a position to meet me, but I'm quite sure I shall find my own way to their house.'

'Okay, ma'am. I hope you enjoyed your flight – good luck with the baby.'

Victoria rubbed her bump lovingly. She waited for the men to disembark before she attempted to follow them. She only had her holdall to bring and her embroidered shoulder bag with all her documents and papers. When she emerged into the sunlight she caused a minor sensation. The two GIs waiting to come aboard to unload the freight gaped at her.

'Gee, we didn't know you were on board, ma'am.

Here, let me give you a hand. It's a long way down for a lady in your condition.'

The short, dark-haired young man took her arm and escorted her from the end of the ramp as though she were an octogenarian not a fighting fit young woman of twenty-three.

Tactfully she disengaged her arm. 'Thank you so much, but until two weeks ago I was a nursing sister in a field hospital on the front line. I'm not nearly as delicate as I look.'

The men exchanged glances, and their attitude changed from friendly to respectful. 'We've heard about the nurses in the field hospitals, ma'am. Our guys owe their lives to ladies like you.'

The second of the young men turned and waved to a passing jeep, which swung in a smooth curve and screeched to a halt beside them. 'Here, Joey, give this lady a ride back to the office, will you? She's just back from the Burma front.'

This time no one offered to help her into the vehicle, and she jumped in and settled herself beside the driver. 'I don't know why everyone is so surprised; after all, I am wearing my uniform, and my status and rank are clearly marked on my shoulder.'

Instantly the GI snapped to attention. 'Sorry, ma'am. Not used to female officers on this airbase.'

Frustrated that he'd misinterpreted her comment as a reprimand she tried to explain. 'There's no need for formality – I'm no longer an officer. I was discharged as unfit for duty. I just haven't had the opportunity to purchase any mufti yet.' She glanced at her bulging midriff and smiled at the driver.

'Gee, ma'am, I guess you must have married one of our guys out there.'

'I certainly did. Captain Taylor King is my husband and I'm going to join his family at a place called Beacon Hill in Boston. Is Boston far from here?'

'Well, this is Dorval airbase and it's in Canada. Boston isn't far away – not really. You can catch the train, but I guess it'll take a few hours. If you're lucky and there's one running this afternoon, you'll be there by late evening.'

Victoria glanced around. So this wasn't America; she was in yet another foreign country. Well, Canada was British really, but surely these men were Americans, not Canadians?

'Will there be a telephone I can use in the administration building, do you think?'

'Sure thing, ma'am. If your folks are expecting you, they'll be waiting to get your call.'

The administration building was quiet. No more transport or other planes were expected that day. No one checked her papers, and in spite of the fact she was an alien in their midst she was more or less ignored. Well, she had had to find her way from London to Essex all those years ago, so she was quite sure she could organise her own transport to the station.

She approached an officer who was staring at a list of names on his clipboard. 'Excuse me, Captain, but I need transport to the nearest train station. Could you please direct me to somewhere I can find a taxi or bus?'

For a moment the man stared open-mouthed, then he swallowed and a faint blush crept up his cheeks. 'Well, ma'am, I'd be proud to give you a lift myself. I'm going into town almost immediately. How about you come with me and get settled somewhere comfortable and I'll come and collect you when I'm ready to go?'

What a very nice man. 'Actually, I would like to use the restroom, if there is one here.' She saw the look of horror on the man's face. 'Please, don't worry if it's fairly basic. I've just come back from five months on the Burma-India front and whatever your facilities, they have to be better than the ones we had there.' The captain's eyes crinkled. 'On the Burma front you say, ma'am? You're the first person I've met who's actually been out there. Is it as bad as they say? It sounds as hot as hell.'

'It's certainly hot, and it's the monsoon at the moment, so it's very wet as well. But, like everything else, you get used to it in time.' She looked around, her condition making the need for the lavatory urgent. 'Captain, the restroom?'

He led her to a door, first beckoning to a couple of air crew lounging about with cigarettes in their hands by an open door. 'You two, get over here and check the restroom's empty, then stand guard whilst this lady uses the facilities.'

Cigarettes were stamped on and they responded to his orders with alacrity. She was amused to find her presence caused such a stir; there must be a lack of women in this vicinity. Maybe the fact that her pregnancy had added a glow to her cheeks and that her hair, which hadn't been cut for several months and now curled over her collar, had something to do with it. The four weeks she'd spent eating well and relaxing since coming out of the jungle had added an extra half a stone to her usually slender frame. Even in her faded battledress she supposed she might be considered a beautiful woman.

The facilities were no worse or better than she expected. Over the past year she'd learnt to hold her breath when necessary and keep her eyes firmly to the front. She washed her face and hands and ran her fingers through her hair and was then ready to rejoin her escort.

Outside, the two men sprang to attention and she was forced to salute. Grinning at them, she explained she was no longer a serving officer and they could relax. 'As long as you're in uniform, ma'am, you'll get the respect you deserve. Captain Frazer has asked us to take you to the cafeteria; you can get a coffee and something to eat whilst you wait.'

Taylor had told her not to expect tea to be offered. Americans preferred to drink coffee and didn't even have milk. A strong cup of black coffee was exactly what she needed to wake her up. It seemed she had several more hours to travel before she reached her destination.

She fortified herself with two mugs of black coffee, and a curious mixture of small pancakes, maple syrup and crisp bacon. She'd been about to refuse the bacon – she never ate pork under any circumstances – but it smelt so tasty and had been served with such loving attention, she could at least pretend to eat it. Her father would have been horrified to see her clean plate, but she'd enjoyed every mouthful. Somehow her lifelong adherence to vegetarianism had become less important. When you needed to eat in order to stay alive you stopped worrying about whether it was fish or fowl and just ate it.

Victoria looked round. It was strange to see so many pale, plump faces – nowhere were there the battle-hardened, lean and hungry-looking men she'd met everywhere in India. She supposed these men had been deemed unfit for active duty and remained at home servicing the planes and doing all the other things that kept the war machine running smoothly.

Feeling better than she had for weeks, she reached into her shoulder bag and withdrew her journal. In it, she'd written the full address of the place she was going and the telephone number. She was tempted to send Mrs King a cable, as it seemed telegrams were called over here, but that would be cowardly. She must introduce herself, let them know she wasn't going to allow them to push her into a subservient position and let them take over her child.

She'd already written to her bankers and lawyers in England. She'd done this as soon as she was married so there would already be ample funds waiting for her at the bank in Boston Taylor had told her the family owned.

She beckoned to a passing GI. 'Excuse me, I need

to make a phone call. Could you tell me where I might find a telephone that is available to civilians?'

The young man shook his head. 'I don't know, ma'am. I guess there's a phone in the major's office, but I don't know if he'll let you use it. I can show you where his office is if you like?'

She stood up. 'I just have to pay for my meal, and then I'll come with you, thank you.'

He looked puzzled. 'You don't have to pay, ma'am – the meal's on us. All the guys here are real pleased to be able to give back just a little something to someone who's done so much for our buddies out there.' She glanced around to see the smiling faces of several men.

It seemed she was no longer invisible. Her appearance had been noted and appreciated. Good, this might mean the commanding officer, whoever he might be, would be more amenable to her request to use his precious telephone.

That proved to be the case; Major Bristow was delighted to vacate his office for a few moments so she could make the call in private. After a deal of whirring and clicking and speaking to operators she was finally told she was connected to the number she required. She could hear the buzz-buzz and waited, her hands clammy on the receiver, for it to be picked up.

'The King residence.'

This wasn't one of her relatives: the voice had a decided drawl to it, not the slight twang she'd come to expect from a Bostonian. 'Good afternoon, I would like to speak to Mr or Mrs King. It's Victoria King here, Taylor's wife.'

'I'm sorry, ma'am, there's no one at home today. Mrs King is spending the day at the country club and Mr King is downtown at work.'

Victoria stared at the phone in astonishment. The speaker, presumably a servant, showed little interest in her arrival. She'd expected more reaction than that; after all Taylor, according to him, was the blue-eyed boy, the heir to all he surveyed. There was something very odd about this.

'I see. I don't know exactly when I shall be arriving in Beacon Hill. However, could you please inform them that I shall definitely be there later this evening. Presumably they will both be home then?'

'No, ma'am, they have a dinner engagement this evening. It might be better if you booked into a hotel tonight.'

She slammed the phone down. Were her mother and father-in-law so disinterested in their son's new wife that they wouldn't give up a dinner engagement? This was not a good start. She hadn't even taken her first step on American soil or spoken to her new in-laws. In fact, she was still in Canada and had another hundred or so miles to travel before she reached the place she would be calling home in future. She was not to be welcomed, but forced to stay in a hotel in order to arrive at a time convenient to Mr and Mrs King. She already hated her in-laws.

6

HOSTILITIES BEGIN

Victoria decided she would go to the address in Louisburg Square whatever time she arrived. Taylor would be horrified to think of her staying unaccompanied in a strange hotel when she could be sleeping comfortably in his apartment at the family home.

Her journey was uneventful; the amount of space inside and the punctuality of her train amazed her. There might have been no war on. For the bulk of Americans the fighting was so far away it had little to do with their daily lives, unless of course, they had sons, husbands or fathers overseas.

Here there was no rationing, no shortage of anything and the shops were bursting with items she had only dreamt about in war-torn London. A little after seven o'clock in the evening she stood outside South Station in Boston looking for a taxi. A porter hailed one for her and she tipped him generously. Taylor had given her a wad of dollars before they parted just in case she had to come home before him.

When she told the driver her address he regarded her with something approaching awe. 'Louisburg Square, ma'am? That sure is a grand place to be going.'

Victoria smiled at his Irish accent. So far she'd heard so many different pronunciations of the English language she was having difficulty adjusting. 'Yes, I believe it is a good part of town. Will it take long to get there?'

'No, ma'am, about twenty minutes is all.'

The taxi followed the traffic past impressive buildings and smart people. When they reached Beacon Hill the houses began to look familiar, like places she'd seen in England. Taylor had told her the city had been founded in the seventeenth century by Puritans from East Anglia. There were still buildings around that had been built then, and unlike some other parts of America, this place was steeped in history.

Eventually the car pulled up in front of an imposing four-storey, brick-built house with green louvred shutters at all the windows. There were scrubbed granite steps leading to the front door. She scrambled out of the taxi and paid the driver. She watched him drive away and mentally crossed her fingers, praying she hadn't made a mistake and that whoever opened the door would let her in. This house was one of many; they all faced inward around a pretty garden. She thought it might be a communal one for the sole use of the residents of the square.

She ran up the steps and hammered loudly on the door. She waited several minutes before footsteps approached. The door swung open and a butler dressed in a black frock coat and a cravat, like something out of a Jane Austen novel, stared at her in astonishment.

She didn't give him a chance to speak but stepped around him. 'Good evening, I am Mrs Taylor King. Kindly show me to my apartment.'

The man recovered his *sangfroid* and actually bowed. 'We were not expecting you tonight, madam, but if you will come this way, I shall take you to Mr Taylor's rooms.'

He marched across the parquet-floored entrance hall and turned sharply to the left. They traversed a long, wide corridor, again with parquet floor and no carpet, until they reached a break in the wall and a flight of steps leading upwards. The butler took the stairs, not looking behind to see she was following, and ascended looking neither to the right nor the left.

At the top of the stairs was a shallow landing and a pair of double doors. He opened them and stepped back.

'These are Mr Taylor's apartments, madam. Will you be requiring anything else tonight?'

There were a lot of things Victoria required and the first of these was the bathroom. 'No, thank you, good evening.' She stepped back smartly and closed the door in his supercilious face.

Wherever had they got that man from? He was more English than she was. Taylor had insisted Americans didn't go in for aristocracy and social mores but obviously in this household things were different.

She should have asked where the bathroom was before slamming the door and now she would have to find it for herself. Dropping her bag on a side table she tried the first of the closed doors. This was the kitchen. She tried the one opposite – that was a study. She worked her way along the corridor until she came to a large bedroom, which had two doors leading from it. Surely one of these had to be a bathroom.

She ran across, her need becoming desperate.

Here was a bathroom as luxurious as the one she'd had at Marpur. She decided to have a long soak in the enormous, claw-footed bathtub. She turned the tap, checking there was hot water, and after a few hisses and gurgles it gushed out, filling the room with steam.

Emerging from her hour-long soak, her hair wrapped in a fluffy white towel and dressed in one of Taylor's bathrobes, she felt ready for anything. She thought her next port of call should be the kitchen. She was starving. She hadn't eaten since she'd had a sandwich hours ago.

The kitchen was the first door on the left after the front door and she had no difficulty retracing her steps. Inside was a revelation. Everything was electric and smooth and sleek, and the refrigerator was big enough to sit in. Unfortunately, it was also switched off and empty. However, a search revealed coffee and she soon had the percolator bubbling on the stove. She had a pack of K-rations for emergencies and she collected them from the hall table.

The drawing room was at the rear of the house and overlooked a pretty garden. The room was well appointed, but not luxurious by any means. In fact, it rather reminded her of The Rookery in Essex, expensive furniture that had seen better days, but it was comfortable and more than large enough for the two of them.

Her fingers splayed across her belly and her mouth curled. There would be three of them when the baby came next April. Her happiness faded as she remembered Taylor was unlikely to be home before the baby arrived. She would be living here for the foreseeable future without him. At least she had her own rooms and need not mix with Taylor's inhospitable parents.

* * *

Victoria slept until late morning, her long journey and pregnancy finally catching up with her. Sleeping in Taylor's bed was perfect; her past was behind her and she was ready to embrace another new life.

The sunlight pouring into her bedroom eventually woke her up. For a moment she was disorientated, not sure where she was. She remained still, eyes open, staring around the room. At the moment things were unfamiliar, but soon it would seem like home.

She scrambled out of bed and made a dash for the bathroom. As there was no food in her apartment she would have to go out to eat. K-rations were all very well in an emergency, but she craved something more substantial, something like a plate of those small golden pancakes dripping with maple syrup and crisp bacon on the side. Her stomach gurgled in anticipation of the treat.

Dressing quickly in her clean uniform she put her documents and a wad of notes into her shoulder bag.

She wondered if there was a back exit, one that she could use to avoid the main part of the house. Feeling like an intruder, she slipped the key from the inside of the door and carefully locked the apartment behind her. Now she was in residence she didn't want anyone else going in.

She tiptoed down the stairs, closing her eyes at the bottom in order to visualise the route she'd taken the previous day. She'd turned right at the stairs so perhaps if she continued to the left she would find a secondary door leading out to the street. For some reason she didn't want to meet Taylor's parents wearing her tatty uniform, even though it was proof that she was more than just a wife. She wanted to turn herself back into a civilian, emphasise her maternity, become someone who fitted more easily into these palatial surroundings.

The house was silent even though it was almost midday, but the space being so large she doubted if she'd hear anyone in the main part of the house anyway. The passage ended at a large door with substantial bolts. This had to be an external door as it had so many security devices.

She looked nervously in both directions, not wishing to be caught creeping out like a thief. The bolts grated and the noise echoed down the empty corridor. She glanced back, checking, but no one appeared to accuse her of wrongdoing. Ten minutes later she was outside the front, beside the granite steps. This time she noticed there was an old-fashioned foot scraper; this too was painted a smart green like the door and shutters.

The pavement – sidewalk was what she would have to call it now – was immaculate and all the other houses had doors painted black or dark green and most of them had the same red bricks and shutters matching their doors.

She didn't have a map of the area, but she had a good memory and could find her way back down the street and to a department store, as Taylor had told her shops were called over here. Leaving Louisburg Square, she turned left into Mount Vernon Street. There were a few people walking and none of them appeared to notice her, for which she was grateful. Taylor had told her that Americans were friendly, so perhaps if she stopped and asked someone where she could find a taxi they would give her directions.

She reached the end of the road and turned right into a road named Joy Street. To her delight she saw a cruising yellow cab and waved vigorously. Immediately it pulled over to the kerb and a friendly face addressed her through the open window.

'Where to, ma'am? It's not often we see combat dress up here on Beacon Hill.'

'I only arrived last night and still have no civilian clothes. Could you take me somewhere I can buy what I need?'

'I know exactly where you want to go, ma'am, Bonwit Tellers – you'll sure get fine frocks there. Are you living up here?'

By this time Victoria was settled comfortably on the back seat. 'Yes, Louisburg Square.'

The man whistled through his teeth, obviously impressed. 'Then in that case, you'll certainly want to go to Bonwit Tellers to shop.'

As they drove down towards the centre of town she watched out of the window, drinking in the differences, the wide sidewalks, some of brick, not flagstones. Pedestrians were casually dressed, neither smart nor shabby. The men wore crumpled suits made of a light cotton material. She'd discovered several hanging in Taylor's wardrobe.

The cars she saw in Beacon Hill were not large, not like the Bentley Arthur had driven. It seemed rich Bostonians did not wish to display their wealth. While she was out, she intended to find the bank and get her finances sorted out. She was also going to buy groceries and stock the enormous refrigerator and larder. She had no intention of being beholden in any way to the family she was now connected to. If they made her life too difficult she would find somewhere else to live. She had enough money to do that, but until Taylor returned she really ought to stay where she was.

It was late afternoon before she'd completed her purchases, visited the bank and been to the nearest grocer's. Her account had already been set up as instructed by her English bankers, and she had a satisfactory amount of money available, far more than she could spend in a year. The wad of dollars Taylor had given her had covered today's purchases and she still had quite a lot left over.

The grocer's shop, she was told it was called a *deli*, was delighted to have a customer at such a prestigious address and the owner had helped with her selections. He had promised the food would be delivered before five o'clock.

Now in a floral smock, cotton slacks, comfortable flat shoes and a smart new bag over her shoulder, she felt ready to meet Mr and Mrs King. The taxi dropped her at the front door and she ran up the steps. It was ridiculous she had to knock like a visitor but she didn't feel comfortable just walking in.

She rapped the brass knocker and waited for the absurd butler to appear. The door was opened by a smiling black woman in a smart maid's uniform. 'Oh my, you must be Mr Taylor's new wife. We wondered where you'd got to. Madam and Sir are in the drawing room. Would you like to go straight there, ma'am?'

Well, this was a change from last night. 'Yes, thank you. I'm sorry if I've worried anyone; I had to go into town. By the way, there will be a delivery of groceries coming. Could you possibly put them in my apartment?' She rummaged in her bag and held out the key. 'I've locked the door, so whoever takes them will need this.'

The maid shook her head. 'No, ma'am, there's a key to the apartment hanging on the wall in the kitchen. You keep yours.'

This news didn't please Victoria. If there was a key available to the staff, that must also mean her in-laws could come and go as they pleased. She valued her privacy; she didn't want to think of people prowling around in her private domain when she was absent. She walked across the slippery floor towards the imposing double doors, which the maid opened for her.

'You just go on in, ma'am; they'll be expecting you.'

Victoria stepped through the door and stared down the room, which stretched from the front to the back of the house. Standing in front of an impressive array of modern art was a tall, thin man the image of her husband.

Her lips curved, and he responded. 'Come in, my dear, we must apologise for being out when you arrived last night. If we'd known you were coming we would have made sure your icebox was full and your apartment more welcoming.'

She walked gracefully across the expanse of grey carpet and offered her hand. 'I had some rations left over from the battlefront, Mr King, and there was coffee in the cupboard. I managed quite well, thank you.'

He grasped her hand in both of his and squeezed it gently. She saw his eyes were moist as he glanced down at her bump. 'We were delighted when our son cabled us with the news that you're expecting his child, my dear girl. We have other grandchildren, but they don't have our name.'

Victoria withdrew her hand, chilled by his casual comment. She turned to greet the woman, who had not risen from the armchair she'd been sitting in.

'Mrs King, Taylor has told me so much about you; I hope we can be friends.'

Victoria had been about to step forward and offer her hand, thinking perhaps her mother-in-law was infirm, and unable to rise. She was glad she hadn't. She was pierced by an antagonistic glare. This woman was dressed from the same store she'd bought her clothes – she recognised the outfit – and wore her hair swept back in an elegant chignon. Her face was discreetly made-up, but there was no smile of welcome.

For a horrible moment Victoria's words hung in the air unanswered. Then slowly the woman rose and she could see she was as thin as her husband and almost as tall.

'When is the baby due, Victoria?'

Startled by the abrupt question Victoria froze, unable to remember her due date. 'Sometime in April, Mrs King.' She added nothing else.

'And you were married, when?' The slight emphasis on the last word made her cheeks burn.

'The baby was conceived on our honeymoon, Mrs King, not before.' How dare the woman ask such a question? It was none of her business.

'That is a relief, I must say. I have to tell you, Victoria, this whole business has been a shock to me. Taylor had an understanding with the daughter of a dear friend of mine. Rebecca Searle is devastated and so are her parents.' The woman's nostrils flared and she tilted her head, as if detecting a bad smell.

She was dismissed. She turned to glance at Mr King, hoping he might step in and defuse the poisonous atmosphere, add more words of welcome. But during the brief exchange with her mother-in-law he had vanished. She saw the door at the end of the drawing room swing shut.

So, that's how things were in this house. Taylor's father made himself scarce when there was trouble. She knew she could expect no support from him. Well, she'd faced far worse on the front line and she wasn't going to let this obnoxious woman destroy her happiness.

'That's unfortunate, but not my concern. Taylor and I met, fell in love and got married and we're having a child. That is what you should consider carefully, Mrs King. If you wish to remain in contact with your only son and his child I suggest...' She paused, not sure what she was going to suggest, then something prompted her to say: 'Then I suggest you don't mention Rebecca whatever her name is, in my presence again. I'm not sure if you are aware, but I have sufficient funds of my own to be totally self-supporting. I shall only remain under your roof as long as it suits me.' She turned and, parade-ground stiff, stalked down the length of the room and out.

Her fury kept her going until she was safely inside her apartment, but then she started to shake and a wave of nausea overtook her. She barely reached the bathroom in time before being horribly sick.

She had sat down to write to Taylor, tell him what had happened, but tore the letter up. He was still fighting, his life in danger – the last thing she wanted was for him to be worried about her. She looked around the clinical kitchen; it needed a few personal items to cheer it up. She would buy some colourful plates and mugs, and flowers. She'd not seen flowers anywhere in the house and she was not surprised.

The friendly maid who had let her in earlier brought up the groceries. Dolores was quite happy to stand and chat for a while. From her she learnt the best places to visit, where to eat out, and how to call a taxi to the house. There was a park nearby called, simply, Public Garden, and also another green area called Boston Common. Perhaps once she had explored the neighbourhood she would feel more relaxed. After meeting her in-laws she doubted that she would ever call Louisburg Square her home.

She busied herself filling up the cupboards and refrigerator. She had no appetite, still felt slightly nauseous, but must eat if she was going to remain healthy and do the best for her baby.

7

THIEVES

Victoria settled into her new life, but wasn't happy. Her in-laws ignored her, failing to include her in any invitations or inviting her to dine with them. If it hadn't been for Dolores she would have had no one to talk to.

She had been unable to go out and explore as fresh snow had fallen. She hated the cold weather; it reminded her of England and what she'd left behind there. How had she ended up living somewhere with the same inhospitable climate? And, as before, she was trying to survive without the man she loved, but at least in England she had been welcome. She couldn't help contrasting Marion and Arthur's greeting to the chilly reception she had received from her new in-laws.

She discovered the whereabouts of the local doctor and when the streets were cleared decided to venture into town in order to register.

The interior of the building was clinical, but the crisply uniformed receptionist greeted her enthusiastically.

'Good morning, how can I help you, ma'am?'

'I am Mrs Taylor King and I would like to register with Doctor Middleton.' As expected, mentioning Taylor's name had a magical effect and the paperwork was completed with the minimum of fuss. She was offered coffee and pastries but refused. After a brief wait another uniformed young lady appeared and called her through.

Doctor Middleton examined her. 'The baby, as I am sure you are aware, Mrs King, is due in the middle of April. You are fit and healthy and I don't anticipate any problems with the remainder of this pregnancy. However, you are a little underweight and I would like you to increase your daily consumption.'

'I am eating healthily, but my appetite is small. Thank you for seeing me so promptly.'

'My pleasure, ma'am. I shan't need to see you

again until March unless, of course, you have any problems.'

She thanked him again and left with the usual pile of leaflets and forms one would expect for a first confinement. She stood in the waiting area and flicked through, checking that she had everything she needed. Although it was cold the sun was out and she decided to remain in town for lunch. After all, there was nothing in her apartment to draw her back.

Maybe there would be another letter from Taylor – they tended to arrive in batches even though they had been posted separately. The last one had told her that the Japanese were on their last legs. In some places he'd heard they were eating their own boots and rats as well, but they refused to surrender.

He thought the war in the Pacific wasn't going to end as rapidly as the one in Europe, which was drawing to a definite close. The Allies were moving inexorably through France and Germany whilst the Russians were closing in from the north. Victoria had heard on WORL, the local radio station, that victory in Europe was expected before the summer. She prayed they were correct.

When she wrote to him, or her parents, she didn't say just how miserable she was, or how lonely and unloved in the so-called 'land of the free'. For her,

America might be a new country, but it wasn't one she was comfortable in.

Even Taylor's sisters had not bothered to come around and introduce themselves. They lived out of town, in a place called Prides Crossing on the north side. If they had wanted to meet her, they could have made the effort even when the weather was poor. No one, not even any of the friends Taylor had spoken about so enthusiastically, made themselves known to her. After spending so many years surrounded by friendly faces the isolation was making her depressed.

The deli she'd discovered in Charles Street continued to deliver her weekly groceries, but she found it difficult to eat. Cooking had never been something she enjoyed and often she existed on a diet of fruit and bread and cheese. Dolores brought this to a close. She was in the apartment doing a daily tidy when she made her suggestion.

'You need someone to look after you, ma'am. I don't reckon you're eating properly and you sure aren't cooking yourself a hot meal every day.'

'Do you know someone who would come in and do that?'

Dolores nodded. 'My daughter Rose, ma'am. She lives with me and her last position has just ended. Her folks have moved away like a lot of them are at the moment. Like you she's married and her man's overseas. He's in the air force. I just know she'd be glad to help out.'

'Then please ask her to come. Can she start tomorrow morning?' Victoria was certain any relative of Dolores would suit her. She'd become fond of the cheerful black lady over the past difficult weeks.

The next morning her new housekeeper reported for duty wearing the same formal black and white her mother did.

'Rose, I'm so pleased to meet you. Did your mother tell you what I need doing?'

'Yes, ma'am, she did. Cleaning, laundry and cooking – in fact anything that you want.'

'That's wonderful. And tomorrow please don't wear that uniform. I much prefer you to wear something comfortable and bring an apron if you must.'

The young woman grinned. 'Mom said I was to put this on, but I don't like it. I'll be glad to wear my own clothes to work. I can promise you I'll work just as hard whatever I'm wearing.'

Victoria was warming to this sparky young woman. She was of a similar height to her mother but half her weight. But she too had the tight black curls and coal-black skin that seemed to make her face glow with an inner light.

It was better having someone in her own employ. She'd always felt Mrs King was grudgingly allowing her the services of Dolores.

'Rose, I'm so glad you're here. I'm absolutely useless when it comes to domestic chores. Can I leave everything to you? If you work out how many hours you think you need to do, just let me know what I owe you.'

'I sure am grateful for this chance, Mrs King. I'll work whenever you like, even at weekends if you want me to. Where shall I start this morning?'

Having someone about the place made her feel less alone. She was breaking all the rules by making friends with Rose and Dolores, but her stint as a nurse in London, and then overseas with the Queen Alexandra's nurses, had changed her attitude. Those she used to think of as the *lower classes* were in fact exactly the same as she was. The only difference was money.

There were no barriers; they were artificial. All people had been made in God's image regardless of creed, colour or background and all required the same amount of love and encouragement to survive in this harsh world. She didn't care if the Kings and their snooty friends disapproved; in fact it only reinforced her determination to continue the friendship.

On Sunday she was expected to accompany Mr

and Mrs King to their local church and pretend she was part of the family. This was the only time they did anything together and even then she was rarely introduced to other members of the congregation. Her mother-in-law told everyone that Victoria was not socialising until after the baby was born.

Surely there must be other young women in a similar situation as hers? However, not even they made any overtures of friendship. Taylor talked enthusiastically in his regular and loving letters about *baby showers* where all one's friends came around with gifts for the new arrival. So far the only things she'd got for the forthcoming arrival she'd had to buy for herself.

It had become clear to her that she was viewed as an interloper, an aberration, Taylor's alien wife – someone who existed, but would never be part of their lives. Was it because she was so dark? All the families she'd seen so far were universally tall, pale, and with washed-out blue eyes and streaky fair hair. She knew her in-laws wished Taylor had married Rebecca whatever her name was, and perhaps still hoped he would.

Something happened towards the end of March that made her decide the time had come to find somewhere else to live. She had had the locks on her apartment changed and only Rose and she had keys. She had also offered to pay rent to Mr King, but he had been offended at her suggestion.

Rose had started to accompany her when she went out. The pavements were slippery and Victoria felt she needed an arm to lean on. One morning she decided to reduce her daily walk to a brief stroll round the park in the centre of Louisburg Square. When she informed Rose of her decision the girl was delighted.

'I'm sure glad of that, ma'am.' Despite her pleas Rose steadfastly refused to call her by her first name.

'Good – I was in danger of becoming predictable. We have been walking out together at ten o'clock every morning and always take an hour to do it. It's high time I changed my routine.'

They set off as usual at ten o'clock but instead of heading for Boston Common they crossed the road and went into the private park that ran down the length of the square. They returned after twenty minutes from the short, brisk walk, entering the house in the usual way through the door at the end of the corridor. 'My, Mrs King, it sure is cold today. I reckon it's going to snow again. At least it's warm inside.'

'Well, Rose, I have no reason to go out again. I can write my journal, read my books, and listen to the radio until the weather improves.'

'You know what they say in Boston, ma'am. If you

don't like the weather – wait a minute and it'll change. So if it snows today, tomorrow it'll be sunny again.'

Laughing together they headed along the passageway and turned to go up the stairs. Victoria stopped – shocked. 'The door to the apartment is open. Could we have forgotten to lock it when we went out?'

Rose shook her head, her expression concerned. 'You wait here, ma'am. I'll go up and see who's in there.'

She leaned against the wall, one hand on the banister, and watched Rose tread quietly to the open door. She knew she should stay where she was, but something urged her on. This was her house, her home, and if there were burglars she wanted to see for herself.

Pulling herself upright with some difficulty, she followed up the stairs and into the apartment. She came face to face with her mother-in-law and another woman, who could only be Taylor's younger sister because the girl looked so very like him. Victoria didn't know which of the intruders was more surprised, or embarrassed, by the confrontation.

'What the hell are you doing in my apartment? How did you get in here? You have absolutely no right to be in my home.' Her tone was strident, but she couldn't help herself. The repressed resentment was bubbling up inside her – the weeks of being ignored, being treated like someone undesirable, made her forget to keep her head down, to accept the invasion of her privacy with dignity.

Mrs King and her daughter took two involuntary steps backwards, sensing her barely suppressed rage.

'We were just leaving. You might consider this is your apartment, Victoria, but it is not. This is my house, and I have every right to visit anywhere I wish to. It is you who are the intruder.'

Victoria advanced, murder in her eyes. 'I'll say it again. You have no right to be here. I offered to pay rent for the apartment but Mr King refused. This is Taylor's personal space. Would you have broken in here, like thieves, if he was here? I don't think so. I think you're both despicable. How someone as kind and intelligent as Taylor comes from this family is beyond me. He is everything that you're not.' She paused, glaring at the two cowering women. 'He is a gentleman. He will be appalled when I tell him what you have done and how I've been treated these past weeks.' Slowly she raked them from the toes of their court shoes to the crowns of their professionally coiffured heads, making her disdain apparent.

'You two are worse than burglars. You are dishonest, inhospitable, unpleasant and I want you to get out of my apartment right now.'

The two women scuttled past, pressing their backs to the wall as they did so. A triumphant flood of adrenalin surged around her body. For the first time she had made herself visible. It felt so good to be in charge of her destiny again. Mrs King hated her, had no intention getting to know her better. She would find somewhere else to live, somewhere away from this pernicious woman.

She swayed, reaction setting in. Rose slipped her arm around her waist and helped her to the drawing room.

'There, you sit down and I'll fetch you a nice cup of coffee.'

Victoria leant back and the dizziness passed. Taylor would be horrified she'd fallen out so publicly with both his mother and sister. She supposed it was his sister; she hadn't given the woman time to introduce herself.

Far too late to worry about that. She'd burnt her boats – all she had to do was find somewhere else to live. There was no way on this earth her next child was going to have any contact with Taylor's horrible family. She no longer cared if her husband disapproved. He could come with her, or remain with his family, but she was not staying a minute more than she had to.

A wave of nausea engulfed her. Did this really mean the end of her marriage? She remembered the old adage: *Marry in haste and repent at leisure.* Was this to be her fate? The last few months she'd had plenty of time to repent, but had suppressed her feelings of despair in case they overwhelmed her. She knew in wartime emotions were heightened; people did things they would not normally contemplate. The reality was that their grand passion was looking decidedly shaky.

Rose appeared with a steaming mug of coffee, well laced with sugar, and handed it to her, before sitting down beside her. 'There, drink this. I don't know how Mrs King and Mrs Robinson got in here. I've never given them my key; I can only think Teddy, the man who changed the locks, must have given them one.'

She stared at Rose. 'What are you saying? That they could have been in and out of here all the time and I never knew until today?'

Rose nodded. 'I reckon so, ma'am; she's always been cunning, that one. She had plans for her son, and they didn't include you. She would be glad to see your marriage over before it's begun.'

A wave of misery swept over her. Had she given Taylor's mother the victory she so wanted? She closed her eyes and tears trickled down her cheeks. No, she couldn't believe her marriage was over. Taylor's letters were full of love, full of encouragement, and in spite of their brief time together, she knew him as well as she'd known Henry. The baby inside her kicked vigorously and hot coffee slopped into her lap.

Smiling, she handed her mug to Rose. 'It's a good thing I'm still wearing my coat or this little baby would have had a nasty surprise.' She heaved herself up from the sofa and quickly unbuttoned it. 'Rose, I need to go downtown to see the real estate agent. I want to find somewhere to live and move out of here by the end of the week.'

* * *

Three days later she had all her belongings neatly stacked in boxes. Her books, the gramophone and records, the radio, her plants and ornaments as well as the baby things, were ready to be carried out to the waiting removal van. Victoria had found a lovely house to rent in Marlborough Street. There were three floors, more than enough space for what she wanted.

She invited Dolores and Rose to move into the self-contained apartment at the top of the building and they accepted with alacrity. She knew Dolores was a widow, and her two sons, as well as her son-in-law, were serving overseas.

She looked around the apartment for the last time, feeling absolutely no regrets to be leaving. She hadn't seen Mrs King since the altercation; in fact she hadn't seen anyone at all apart from Rose and her mother. She knew her in-laws must be hoping she was leaving for good. Mrs King would already have written to her son and would expect him to choose his family over his new wife and child. She was confident he would do the opposite.

He'd said, when she had told him she was independently wealthy, that he had no objection to being kept by his wife. It was possible he might be relieved to be away from the emotional austerity of his family home, to be able to live as he chose, to find his own way in the world.

She dropped the two keys on the side table and walked out. She didn't leave a forwarding address.

8

LIKE FATHER

The house in Marlborough Street was only a few hundred yards from the Public Park and ideal for someone about to have a baby. Victoria could still ask Dolores or Rose to order her vegetables and groceries from the same deli in Charles Street. She wasn't any further from the main shopping area downtown either, so it had been an excellent choice.

She had posted a letter to Taylor on the same day she'd had her confrontation with Mrs King but knew it could be several weeks before she got a reply. Quite often their letters crossed, her post still chasing him around the Pacific. She had a feeling he was no longer in the jungle but on a patrol boat flushing out the remaining pockets of Japanese resistance in the islands.

The all-female household was working well. Dolores and Rose were close and were happy to share the comfortable attic apartment. There was more than enough room for Otis, Rose's husband, when he returned, if he returned, Victoria thought, sending a quick prayer skywards.

The losses in the RAF were far worse than for the ground troops. Now the U-boats had been cleared from the seas and the German air force all but defeated, travelling by sea was no longer dangerous either.

She hadn't written to Valerie and the others. Her place would have been filled and she was no longer a part of their lives. She'd learnt over the years to close the door behind her and not look back.

As the days drifted into weeks, her due date rapidly approached. The winter vanished overnight and after barely a week or so of mild spring weather the trees burst into bloom and the weather became humid. She was more at home in the warm humidity than in the icy conditions she had endured since arriving in Boston.

There had not been a word from her in-laws; if they wished to find her they could easily do so, so it wasn't this stopping them from contacting her. The three months living in Louisburg Square might never have taken place. They might reappear in her life when her baby was born, especially if it was the much longed for grandson.

She tottered down to see her doctor and to check that a private room was booked at the clinic. She had been surprised to discover most babies were born in hospital. Home deliveries, it seemed, were only for those who didn't have the wherewithal to pay for the medical care. She thanked God she was not one of those unfortunates.

April drifted in and the baby's head engaged fully; it wouldn't be long before he was born. She was much bigger this time, and was crushed by the weight. Her legs could scarcely hold her up; she expected to buckle at the knees at any time. Staggering around the size of a mountain was decidedly unpleasant. Her ankles swelled if she walked too far, so even the short distance to the Public Garden was no longer possible.

The house she was renting had a pretty backyard, a paved area where you could sit, walls running down either side for privacy, and a grassy area with a child's swing attached to a sturdy tree at the other end. It had been the child's swing that had made her select this particular property.

She was sitting, her feet resting on a footstool,

when Rose came out, her face split by a beaming smile.

'Look, Mrs King, you have three letters. They must've been held up somewhere.'

Victoria's heart skipped, and it wasn't with excitement; she felt a trickle of sweat running down between her shoulder blades, knew her hands were unsteady. She took the three envelopes and flicked through, trying to see if there was a postmark or date that would tell her which one had been written first. They were too smudged and grubby to decipher anything. She selected one and carefully opened it. She pulled out the usual half a dozen pages and looked at the date. This had been written before he could have heard from either her or his mother. She folded the letter and opened the second, looked at the date and braced herself.

She scanned the letter with growing astonishment. It had been written in the usual loving way, asking after her, after the baby, apologising that he wouldn't be there when it was born, saying he thought he would be back by the summer the way things were going. There were several amusing anecdotes about his buddies, as he called them, and she was beginning to think neither letter had arrived, then on the last page he referred to the move.

Victoria darling, forget all about Louisburg Square. I already have. You did the right thing to move away. I half-expected my mother and sisters to behave appallingly – they had set their hearts on a union between Rebecca and I. I never had any intention of marrying her; she's too like me. I've no wish to perpetuate the family customs and snobbery. Marlborough Street is perfect, I know it well. I can't wait to come home and settle in with you and our baby. Please don't worry about my parents and sisters; they'll come around soon enough when the baby is born. And if they don't, who the hell cares? I certainly don't. As long as I have you, I shall be content with life. Take care of yourself, my darling. I miss you.

Your loving husband,
Taylor

Tears rolled down her cheeks, as much from relief as happiness. She had been right; it was no contest really. When Taylor had married her he must have been aware how things would be, so why had he not warned her? If she had known her reception was going to be so frosty, that she would be made to feel like a social pariah, she might well have refused to come to Boston, might have stayed in India until the war was over, regardless of convention.

She wiped her eyes on the floating sleeve of her peignoir. Her initial relief that Taylor considered the move a good thing, and was quite happy to abandon his parents, began to be replaced by a growing feeling of resentment.

Why hadn't he told her about Rebecca, about his mother, before he'd sent her to live with them? There was something decidedly odd about it all – maybe she was being paranoid, looking for secrets and lies where there weren't any. Her mouth twitched. There were more than enough lies and secrets on her side; they really didn't need any on his as well.

That afternoon she developed a low, dragging pain in the small of her back and an unnatural urge to scrub the kitchen floor. She knew what was coming; the first stages of labour had begun. This time she wasn't scared. She knew that what was going to happen would be excruciatingly painful and even more undignified, but it was endurable. The joy of holding her baby in her arms after nine long months would make any amount of discomfort worthwhile. She leant against the large scrub table, hands resting on top of her belly.

'Dolores, I'm in labour. Please call the hospital and

tell them I'm coming. Could you also fetch down the things I need to take with me?'

'I reckon it was the letter from Mr King that started you – nothing like a bit of excitement for bringing on a baby.'

Rose was out. It was her day off and she had gone to visit friends of her husband's; she and Dolores would have to manage on their own. When they arrived at the hospital car park her first strong contraction came. She clenched her teeth and breathed quickly through her nose until it passed. The cab driver opened her door and by the time she had manoeuvred herself out a nurse was waiting with a wheelchair to take her in.

The delivery was mercifully brief, and six hours later Taylor King Junior arrived in the world. All her worries and disappointments evaporated. Her separation from Taylor, her parents, the fact that she'd never see her darling Amelia again – all this was of no importance as she held her son in her arms for the first time.

She stared down at the squalling, red-faced bundle, with joy. He was so different from Amelia – larger, angrier, as if his fight to arrive had made him at odds with the world. She looked down at his little face and smoothed his long black hair. He was so like her own father it broke her heart.

She must ask Dolores to send a cable at once, let him know he had a grandson. Then she bit her lip – she couldn't ask anyone else to send the news – it would have to wait until she was able to do it herself. The baby was taken away from her and placed in the nursery. If she wanted to see him between feeds she would have to ask to be wheeled down the corridor and peer through the window like the doting grand-parents and fathers.

This was unacceptable and she decided to dis-charge herself and take the baby home that very evening. She was a qualified nurse, was more than capable of looking after her own baby, and had no intention of leaving him in the charge of total strangers to cry himself to sleep.

Dolores was on the premises somewhere; she'd promised to wait and see if there was anything she could do. After tying her dressing gown firmly around her waist, she went in search of her. Victoria found her by the water cooler chatting to another visitor.

Dolores jumped up, her face etched with concern. 'Good heavens, ma'am, you shouldn't be wandering about like this. You're supposed to stay in bed, should be in a wheelchair. You only had your baby two hours ago.'

'I know that, Dolores, and I feel fine. I shall rest when I get home. Can you call a cab for us? I've decided to take Taylor Junior back home. I don't like this place; it doesn't suit him or me.'

Dolores exchanged worried glances with the woman she'd been talking to. They obviously believed she'd taken leave of her senses, or that childbirth had made her unbalanced. It was unheard of to leave hospital so soon, or to attempt to walk around on your own two feet as she was doing.

She headed back to her room. By the time she was dressed and her bags packed, she was beginning to wonder if she'd made a sensible decision. She agreed to travel to the taxi in a wheelchair. Perhaps Dolores was right: walking about too much was increasing her blood loss and that wasn't a good idea.

Taylor Junior was in the third crib along and she could see him with his eyes closed and mouth wide open, screaming in protest at being abandoned so soon. Seeing her little son so miserable reinforced her decision to discharge herself.

'Take me in there, please. I'm going to collect my son; he should be comforted, not left by himself with a row of other distressed babies.' They got to the nursery door but were confronted by a starchy sister, outrage on her bony face.

'Mrs King, I'm sorry, but you are not allowed in the nursery. Your baby will be brought to you at the correct time. Kindly return to your room.'

Slowly Victoria pushed herself upright and stepped out of the wheelchair, letting the blanket drop. She saw the sister's shock on seeing her patient was in her outdoor clothes. Victoria wasn't the usual kind of mother; she was someone with a militant gleam in her eye.

'Excuse me, sister, I have come to collect my son. I have decided to go home. I am a fully qualified nursing sister myself, and more than capable of taking care of my baby. I also have two women living in my house, who will give me more support than I shall get here.' She stared imperiously and saw the woman deflate. After all this wasn't a prison; the baby wasn't their property. Victoria dropped back into the wheelchair and Dolores pushed her triumphantly into the nursery.

'Stay where you are, ma'am; I'll collect young sir. Poor little mite, he needs his momma.'

Victoria tucked her baby tenderly into the crook of her arm. He turned his head against her breast, sighed, and fell asleep. She glanced over her shoulder at Dolores and they shared a satisfied smile. Going home, scarcely eight hours after arriving, holding a baby, was quite amazing.

Rose had returned from her day out and answered her mother's knock. She stared down at Victoria, sitting proudly in the taxicab with the unmistakable bundle of a baby in her arms. Dolores grabbed her arm.

'Come along, Rose, we have to get them both back into bed where they belong.'

* * *

Taylor Junior took to the breast with as much gusto as he'd used in screaming when separated from his mother. Victoria watched him sucking greedily and reluctantly admitted the real reason she'd insisted on coming home. She'd left the hospital because she didn't want Mr or Mrs King to see their grandson.

He lay replete in her arms, full of milk, bathed, changed and hopefully ready to sleep for a few hours. She stared down and wondered why her firstborn had been so blonde, so like her English father, whilst Taylor Junior was dark-skinned with black hair like his grandfather. When Taylor saw his son he would know immediately about her ancestry – this baby was so unmistakably not English she was surprised that neither Rose nor Dolores had commented.

The letter had gone to her husband. She'd said they were both well, but that she hadn't informed his parents of the new arrival in their family. He could do that if he wished, but they wouldn't come to her house – even to see a new grandson. If they did her world would fall apart as soon as they saw him, and she wanted Taylor to know before they did.

* * *

The war in Europe finally came to an end at the beginning of May and there were celebrations in the streets, car horns honking, flags flying and strangers hugging each other in excitement. Hitler had committed suicide in his bunker and everyone thought that was too good for him. When the horrific discoveries made in the concentration camps began to filter through, she couldn't bear to read about it and was glad the radio didn't dwell on the horrors.

Hopefully the war in the Pacific would be over soon as well, but the Japanese refused to surrender. They were going to fight to the death, so she was told. So far she hadn't taken her son out to the park but preferred to put him in his stroller in the backyard where he could get all the fresh air he needed and with no one breathing germs as they cooed.

New mothers were expected to remain in hospital for two weeks and she was determined to stay at home until that period was completed. Dolores made sure she did nothing, apart from lie about and feed the baby. Neither of the women had mentioned Taylor Junior's dark skin and long black hair and she was mystified by this. Then when he was two weeks old the explanation became clear. Both women thought he was suffering from jaundice, which yellowed the skin of new-born babies. She didn't wish to disabuse them. She had checked this herself, but the whites of his eyes were clear and the dark skin tone was his natural colour.

It seemed a cruel stroke of fate that her firstborn had appeared petal pink and blonde-haired, the epitome of an English rose, and now she had married into a family of tall, thin aristocratic Bostonians God had chosen to send her a reminder of her past. Taylor wasn't racially prejudiced, he mixed as easily as she had with the Gurkhas and locals, and treated them as he did everyone else. This didn't worry her; it was the fact she had lied to him that weighed her down. If she were to discover that Taylor wasn't the person he'd said he was she would be outraged.

The weather became unpleasantly hot and Dolores told her most of the wealthy decamped from Boston in the summer months and went to live in summer cottages along the Maine coast.

'Do the Kings go away?'

'Oh yes, ma'am, they have a retreat somewhere. They go with all their friends. Mrs King's two daughters and their families go as well. They don't come back until September, when the weather's better.'

'Extraordinary. Do none of the men have to earn a living?'

'Oh yes, the menfolk don't go, or only at weekends, or perhaps the odd week. It's the womenfolk and children who stay down there the whole time. They get brown as berries and come back all the better for it.'

'Have you never been with them? Don't they take the staff?'

'No, the locals look after them; they have a summer staff down there and a winter staff here. We have to find other employment in the summer; that's why they pay such good wages during the winter. It's not quite enough to make up, but it helps.'

Victoria understood now why both women had been so eager to join her. It wasn't just the house; it was the fact that their employment was year-round. 'Well, I'm staying here at least until Mr King returns from the Pacific. I don't mind the humidity and heat, and we have the backyard and the park to get our fresh air.'

Knowing her in-laws had left the city for the next few months was a profound relief. She settled into motherhood happily, revelling in the fact there was no nanny lurking round the corner to snatch the baby away, that she had sole control of his upbringing. After his initial burst of screaming he settled into being a quiet, contented baby, very similar in temperament to Amelia, but there was such a contrast in their looks it was hard to credit they were half-brother and sister.

She had hoped it would be easier when she had another baby in her arms, that the wound inside caused by her separation from her daughter would begin to heal, but it was the reverse. Every time she fed her son she remembered the last time she'd breastfed her daughter and her spirits sunk a little lower.

Conversation with her maids stopped completely and she became more and more withdrawn as the days passed. The news was good but instead of enlivening her, she sank deeper into depression.

She was a nurse, knew what was happening to her, but was unable to prevent herself from becoming unwell. The guilt was tearing her apart inside. She was missing Amelia so much, and having Taylor Junior made her feel the separation more keenly. The baby thrived, unaware of her turmoil.

Victoria soon became isolated from the real world; she no longer noticed what Dolores and Rose were doing and saying. Her whole world revolved around her baby. She could talk to him, but no longer responded to anyone else. She didn't even read the letters that arrived from Taylor and certainly didn't reply.

* * *

Taylor flew in on an overcrowded transport plane at the end of May. He, like the others, was just relieved to be home after so many years fighting overseas. His joy at being back on familiar soil was tempered by concern for his wife. There was something wrong. She hadn't written since the first letter telling him about the birth of his son. She hadn't contacted his parents and they hadn't any idea the child had been born. For some reason he hadn't told them either as he wanted to find out first why Victoria wished to keep the birth a secret.

Was there something wrong with his son? Had

been damaged by his birth? Perhaps her time in the jungle had damaged the foetus. Whatever it was, he would put it right somehow. If things were as bad as he feared he would reassure her, tell her there were homes that could take the child. She didn't have to feel guilty about it, no one would think badly of her for sending away a deformed or damaged child. They could start again and next time they would have a perfect baby.

It took him several hours to get to Boston and unlike Victoria he headed for the T, the subway that was almost as old as the one in London. The distance from the nearest station to Marlborough Street was no more than half a mile. He would enjoy the walk. With his kitbag slung over his shoulder he jogged towards his new home, eager to see his wife and son, but fearing there was something awful awaiting him at home.

9

RENEWAL AND RECOVERY

Taylor paused on the bottom of the steps to stare up at the brick house that was to be his home in future. It wasn't as grand as his parents' house, but for the first time in his life he felt free of restraint, independent, able to make decisions for himself. The problem with being a WASP was that decisions were made by those at the top of the tree; the lower branches were just expected to knuckle down and do as they were told. He sure didn't want to go back to that state of affairs, not having been an officer and having had men under his control, and made life and death decisions for them all, over the past few years.

In spite of his misgivings, he felt liberated, maybe against all the odds he could be happy living in Boston. He knocked lightly on the door and waited for someone to let him in. It seemed real strange having to knock at his own front door.

'Lord have mercy! It's Mr Taylor! Sir, I sure am glad to see you back. Come along in. Mrs King is outside in the yard with the baby.'

Taylor smiled at the large black woman, not recognising her immediately. 'It's Dolores isn't it? You worked for my parents, didn't you?'

'And now I work for you and your wife, sir. My daughter Rose is here as well, and my son-in-law is due to be demobbed any day and then he'll join us.' The woman said this almost defiantly, as if expecting him to object. The more staff Victoria employed the better, as long as he didn't have to organise them or pay their wages. The maid wasn't wearing the neat black and white uniform he'd come to expect. He shrugged; that was his wife's decision also.

Dolores continued. 'We're mighty happy and proud to be employed by such a fine lady and gentleman.'

He detected a certain reservation in her tone, and that sinking feeling came back to him. He was about to blurt his question, ask if everything was okay with his wife and son, but you didn't discuss personal matters with the staff, not even someone like Dolores.

He dropped his kitbag on the parquet floor and nodded towards it. 'There's not much in here I want, but I suppose you'd better launder the clothes and put the rest of the gear in my closet. Did Mrs King bring my clothes with her when she left the square, do you know?'

'Yes, sir, everything's here. All your personal things were packed up and brought down when we moved. Shall I put something out for you? Your rooms are at the back of the house – you can't miss them. They're on the second floor and run the width of the house.'

He nodded his thanks and waited to be directed to the yard. The woman smiled, but it seemed a little forced. 'I'm sorry, sir, I'd forgot that you don't know your way around here. If you go down this passage, the door at the end leads straight out.' Taylor watched her heft the bag over one shoulder and walk easily up the stairs as if it wasn't damned heavy.

He wanted to run outside, sweep his little darling up in his arms and kiss her breathless, but something held him back; some instinct told him that would be the wrong thing to do. She must have heard him coming, heard his voice, but she hadn't rushed out to greet him – the Victoria he'd met and fallen in love with would have done so.

Well, he sure as hell wasn't going to find out what

was wrong by standing around in the vestibule. Squaring his shoulders, he headed for the rear of the house, fixing on a happy smile and determined to keep it there no matter what.

He stepped out into the wet heat and saw, sitting under an awning, a woman he hardly recognised. Could this be his pretty, vivacious wife? Surely not this gaunt woman, her eyes huge and hair cut hideously short? His heart hammered with horror. She resembled one of the photographs he'd seen of an internee from a concentration camp.

Victoria stared at him, but her expression didn't change. She didn't know who he was, but didn't seem to care there was a stranger in the yard with her. She was idly rocking a stroller with one foot and, although he knew he shouldn't, he just had to peep in first before dealing with the catastrophic change in his wife.

'I've been thinking so much about our son, Taylor Junior, sweetheart. Please forgive me, but I must hold him for a moment. I have dreamt of this ever since I received your letter. Let me look at him first and then I shall be all yours.'

At the mention of their son her expression became a little more animated and there was a flicker of life in her eyes, and her lips curved in a facsimile of a smile.

She said nothing, however, but hooked the stroller back with her foot and pushed it in his direction, inviting him to become acquainted with his firstborn.

He braced himself, closing his eyes for a second so whatever he saw wouldn't register on his face. He looked down expecting to see a hideously deformed child, perhaps with missing limbs, with a palsied face; but instead two eyes, exactly the same as his mother's, stared at him from a suntanned face, and the infant waved his arms and smiled.

Taylor was overwhelmed with love. Without hesitation he leant down and scooped the baby up, hugging him, kissing him, as his heart swelled with pride. The baby responded by patting his face as if recognising his father. He knew this couldn't be the case. The baby was scarcely two months old, but he felt a connection. His baby was round, well fed and as healthy and as perfect as any baby he'd ever seen. Had the child drained the life out of Victoria?

If the baby was well, what had caused her to be in this state? Surely the spat with his parents couldn't be the reason for this, whatever it was. He gave his son a final kiss on his soft, floppy black hair and carefully put him back into his stroller. Well, that was one thing out of the way; now all he had to do was find out what was troubling his wife and his life could start getting back to normal.

He sat down next to her and took her hands, shocked at how fragile they were, how the veins showed blue through the translucent skin. God, did she have cancer or some terminal disease? Was that what was wrong and why she looked so ghastly?

'Victoria, darling, tell me what's wrong with you. I know whatever it is we can face it together, but I can't help you if you don't tell me.'

For a moment he felt resistance in her hands, as if she wished to pull away from him, then she spoke to him, her voice scarcely audible. 'What do you think of Taylor Junior?'

Well, that was one question he could answer easily. 'He's one swell little boy. I love him already. He looks just like you, but I don't mind that. I've never much cared for the pale aesthetic look myself.'

He felt the fingers within his own start to tremble, then they shook violently and a noise halfway between a sob and a cough burst from her. Without hesitation he reached out and lifted her onto his lap, rocking her, kissing her gently, mopping her tears as she sobbed as if her heart would break.

He had no idea what this breakdown was all about, but whatever it was, he would sit there and hold her until she was done. She seemed to be responding to him. Perhaps that was all she needed – the support of her husband; after all she was living in a foreign country, amongst unfriendly folk. He should have told her what to expect, should never have sent her back on her own to face the family.

She had seemed invincible in the jungle, but pregnancy could do funny things to a woman. He recalled a school friend whose mom had gone mad after having a baby and her family had had her locked up in an institution for several months.

Finally, the crying stopped and her body went limp in his arms. He pushed away the ratty dark hair and saw she was asleep. At rest her face looked less haggard, a little more like the girl he'd carried in his heart these past few months.

A slight sound caused him to look up and he found both maids hovering by the back door watching him. Their expressions of relief and joy told him all he wanted to know. He stood up, his sleeping wife in his arms, weighing no more than a child now, and carried her upstairs to their rooms. He didn't have to worry about the baby; he felt sure they would take care of him if he cried. The child wasn't his problem now; what he had to do was bring Victoria back from wherever she'd gone, and make her well again.

***

Three months after Taylor's return the weather was so hot and humid, no sooner had she showered than Victoria was damp again. The only thing that made life bearable to those unaccustomed to such humidity was the wind that blew in from the sea.

She wrapped her hair in a towel and, slipping a loose cotton robe over her, emerged from the bathroom to find her husband was awake. He was smiling at her with such love and tenderness in his eyes her heart constricted. How could she have thought he would hate his son and reject her? He hadn't even questioned the baby's dark skin and black hair. He didn't care what his child looked like; in fact he revelled in the fact his parents would be horrified their first King grandson didn't resemble them. Taylor Junior was his son, and that was all that mattered to him.

She returned his smile. His eyes narrowed and he held out his arms in invitation. She couldn't resist. They had only resumed making love recently, and had a lot of time to make up. An hour later she was back in the shower feeling relaxed and well loved. The cubicle door opened and he joined her.

'You can just get out of here, Taylor King. You

know we'll never get showered if you're with me. Remember what happened last time?'

He grinned, looking boyish as his streaky brown hair was plastered over his skull. He slipped his arms around her soap-slippery body. 'I remember perfectly well, darling. We made wild, passionate love.'

'We did not. I trod on the soap and it was a miracle we didn't both break our necks. God knows what would have happened if the cubicle door hadn't burst open.'

He tugged her closer and kissed her hard. 'Nothing is going to happen, not to us, not to our baby. We can get through anything together; we've just proved that haven't we?'

She wriggled free and dodged under the spray to remove the last of the soap. She stepped round him and grabbed a towel, running hastily into the bedroom before he could reach out and draw her back. She heard him laughing and the sound filled her with happiness. There had been a time when she had thought laughter had left their lives forever.

She could hardly remember the black time, the two months after Taylor's birth, when she'd sunk into a depression. This time it hadn't been a jump from half dead to wildly happy and fit. Perhaps the years had taken their toll, although she was not even twenty-five, she'd borne two children, trained as a nurse and spent a year fighting disease and disaster on the front line in the jungles of India.

After unwrapping her towel she stared down critically at her body. She was still too thin, much less of her than there used to be, but her breasts were round and surprisingly firm, her waist tiny, and her flanks regaining their muscle tone. She no longer looked like a starving refugee and felt so much better in herself.

She quickly donned her underwear, a pair of cream linen shorts and a loose, sleeveless cotton top, and then she removed the towel from her head and ran her fingers through her hair. She couldn't remember cutting it off. Dolores had told her she'd done it one night when left on her own. It was growing out now, and with the expert help of the local hairdresser it had shape and looked as though it had been cut short deliberately.

Her husband strode in proudly naked from the shower, not bothering to wrap a towel around his middle as she'd done. He walked into his own dressing room and emerged in shorts and a sleeveless top, similar to the ones she wore.

'I shall be glad when the weather changes next month. Although this isn't as bad as the jungle, I'd forgotten just how enervating the heat is here.'

'I suppose you went down to the coast every year along with your Harvard friends and their families. Did you stay in a huge shingled cottage and sail a yacht?'

'Sure did, honey, and if we're in Boston next year I'll fix something up for us.' Her expression had given her away because he smiled. 'Don't worry, hon, not where my parents or any of the WASPS go – we'll find ourselves somewhere else. There are several artists' colonies around Martha's Vineyard. I'd sure like to spend the summers painting.'

Victoria smiled; this was the first time she'd heard him mention how he wanted to spend the rest of his life, but she approved. He had an allowance from a trust fund, like she did, but until now he hadn't had quite enough money to support himself. However, with the substantial sum she had brought to their joint income they were as well off as many living on Beacon Hill. He had no need to work, no need to pretend to be a banker like his father.

'I hoped you'd make that decision. Why didn't I see anything of yours at your parents' house?'

'Hell, honey, why do you think? They disapprove of my ambition. As you know I kept a visual record of my time in the forces. Some of the images are pretty graphic, so I haven't showed you yet. Would you like to see them?'

She cocked her head, listening to see if Taylor Junior was awake and wanting his bottle. When she'd become so ill her milk had dried up, as it had when she was feeding Amelia, but her son was thriving in the care of four adoring adults.

'Of course I do; I was very impressed with the sketches I saw before. Do you have them in here?' She looked around the room. Where on earth could he have hidden a stack of pictures without them being seen?

He went into his closet and came back with his kitbag. He delved inside and pulled out a bundle of exercise books, two artist's pads, plus pieces of paper and other scraps. He joined her on the bed and without a word dropped them into her lap. She untied the string that held them together and slowly opened the first.

Her heart stilled. She looked at the second and the third and fourth. Staring up at him, her eyes huge, she asked, 'How many of these are of me? They're beautiful. You're truly talented, Taylor. These are even better than the ones I saw. You're a genius, darling.'

The smile he gave her said it all. 'You really like them? I think they're okay, but then I would as they're my work. I wanted to major in art, but like everyone in Louisburg Square, I went to Harvard and majored in business studies.'

She put the portraits of her on one side and then began to look more closely at the others. They were breathtakingly good; although in pencil, they captured the lushness of the jungle, the starkness of battle. Their life together was going to be wonderful. It had bothered her he was so directionless, that he didn't even have an estate to oversee like Arthur and her father. He had no business interests and didn't go down to the bank every quarter to clip coupons like the rich wives Dolores had told her about.

'This is what you must do, Taylor. I think we should leave Boston, go and live on the coast as you suggested next summer, and you must paint. So far you've only drawn. I can only imagine what your work would be like in colour. This is your future, our future. I can't believe it. I'm going to be married to a world-famous artist.'

'Hang on a minute, sweetheart, you're jumping the gun here. I was thinking of painting as a hobby, not a full-time career.'

'Don't you see, darling – it's not good for you to be doing nothing. Everyone needs a focus in life. I've got the house to run, the baby to look after; you must have something purposeful to do as well. And anyway, it would be criminal to allow such talent to go to waste.'

Taylor stared thoughtfully at his drawings, flicking through them, nodding now and again as he recognised their worth. 'I've not used oil paints or watercolours since I was a boy. I'm not sure I could produce what I want in that media. Still, I'll give it a go.'

As he spread out the drawings she realised she was looking at a record of the war as seen by an American officer serving in the Pacific. 'I think we should get these framed and have an exhibition. We can't sell them all, of course, not the ones of me anyway – they're far too personal – but the rest, they're so good they deserve to be out in the world for everyone else to see.'

He shook his head. 'Not these – these are of my buddies, my life. They're not for public view. Some of these guys are dead. How do you think their families would feel seeing the faces of their lost loved ones hanging on a gallery wall?'

'I think they'd be proud, as I would if it had been you. Why don't you take out the ones you don't want to show and give me the rest? I'll make enquiries. I discovered a whole street of art galleries before I stopped going out. When these drawings are mounted and framed I'll take some up there and see what they think.'

She saw him tense, as if he was going to refuse. Then he smiled, and shrugged. 'You go ahead then, honey. If it makes you happy, I'll go along with it.' His eyes suddenly shone with laughter. 'God, imagine how my folks will react when they hear about it? I'll be the black sheep of the family; won't I just love that.'

10

A NEW LIFE

September arrived and Victoria experienced Boston at its best. Cool crisp mornings and evenings, and warm pleasant days; the humidity had gone, along with the high temperatures. Taylor warned her to make the most of it because come November the temperature dropped and it would be below freezing until March or April the following year. There was no need for him to remind her, she had already experienced a bitter winter.

The end of the war meant the pledge that all decent Americans had taken not to buy anything above the legal price limit, appeared to have been abandoned by many stores. As the servicemen returned, pockets bulging with dollars they had been unable to spend whilst in the jungle or the Pacific, prices escalated.

Otis, Rose's husband, joined them, and she liked him immediately. He was as tall as Taylor, but half as wide again, and his skin was a deep bronze. She joked with Rose if she wasn't already deliriously happy with Taylor she might have been looking for a flirtation with her handsome husband.

'Sure, ma'am, you go ahead. My Otis wouldn't notice if you skipped round the house in your underwear. He's a bit slow on the uptake in that direction, and has to be reminded men and women don't just go to bed to sleep.'

Victoria grinned.

'Well I expect that's a relief to you. You don't want to be fighting to keep him at your side every time you go out of the house. Is he going to stay with us, be our chauffeur and handyman, or will he want to find something a little more exciting?'

'No, that's another of his failings – he's sure not too keen on hard work. At least if he's here I can keep him on his toes, make sure he pulls his weight.'

Taylor appeared, his son in his arms, both dressed and ready for their morning constitutional down to the park and around the common.

'Are you both ready at last? I've been standing

down here talking to Rose for the past twenty minutes.'

'Sorry, ma'am. Taylor Junior needed his diaper changing, and it was…'

'I don't wish to know that. As long as he's clean and dry, we can go.'

The pushchair, or stroller as she'd learnt to call it, was waiting in the hall. She watched her husband place his son tenderly inside and strap him in. The baby was now sitting up without support and developing an interest in everything around him. Their daily walks were an important part of all their lives.

Rose held open the front door and Taylor picked the stroller up and carried it down the steps. They had got to know their neighbours, not well, but they nodded and smiled when they went past each other on the sidewalk. In Marlborough Street the air was less rarefied, the people although well-to-do, were not Brahmins. She had been amused to discover this was what they called the elite of Boston.

Taylor loved to push his son in spite of the raised eyebrows and sniggers he got from other men. She had learnt a lot about him in the past few months, things that hadn't been apparent in that brief week they'd spent together in the jungle. Taylor was not at all like his parents.

He was relaxed and easy-going, did as he pleased regardless of convention or current customs. She loved this about him. His disregard for all the things he had been brought up to hold as sacred. They had this in common.

How she longed to be able to tell him about her own break with tradition and reveal she already had a daughter. She thought of Amelia every day and missed her even more since Taylor Junior was born.

'Taylor, Dolores says your parents are back in Louisburg Square. Do you intend to go and see them? They must realise we have a child. Don't you think you ought to take Taylor Junior to meet his grandparents?'

He turned to look at her, his eyes amused. 'You must be kidding? The best thing you ever did, honey, was to mortally offend my folks. I've never been so happy in my life, living here, free of restriction and restraint, not having to go down to the bank and pretend to be working in order to get a handout from my father.'

He stretched out a long arm and hooked her closer, planting a hard kiss on her open mouth. 'And I'm sure glad you persuaded me to have my drawings framed. I hadn't realised I'd done so many, and that they were any good. I'm ready to go with you to the gallery, but if you want to organise it on your own that's fine by me as well.'

Taylor had been unaware his impulsive gesture had been witnessed by several passers-by, none of whom were impressed. Such demonstrations, even in the less hallowed street they were in, were frowned on. She sometimes wished her husband was a little less unconventional.

'I'll give them a call and arrange for us to go and meet the owner. I must say it's made life a lot easier since we bought ourselves a car.'

'And I'm glad we don't have to drive it ourselves. I got my fill of driving in that jeep and vowed never to sit behind the wheel again unless I absolutely have to.'

'Well, I should like to drive. Not many women seem to, but I'm not going to let that put me off. Will you teach me, please? And if we're going to move to a more remote area next spring then I don't want to be dependent on someone else whenever I wish to go out.'

'Sure, honey, I'd love to. We'll get right on to it this afternoon. You won't want to be learning once it freezes.'

They returned from their walk to find the mail had arrived. There was a large pile and Victoria sifted through it eagerly looking for a letter from her parents. She hated having to read this privately, not share the news, but things were going so well between them she didn't want to risk ruining everything by revealing her secrets too soon. She was going to tell him, one day, but not right now.

He thought the letters were from a friend she had made in India, or the mythical friends of her imaginary uncle, and she didn't disabuse him. He'd never suggested she read them out to him; in fact appeared to have no interest in anything she did unless it directly affected his life.

He was a very self-contained man, seemed just as happy on his own as he was with her. The only time he showed real enthusiasm was in bed making love to her or when he was playing with his son. Her lips twitched – and yet he was prepared to kiss her in public. He was a contradiction and she loved him for it.

She thought Valerie might have called him 'a bit of a cold fish', but she thought he was a product of his upbringing. His whole family was reserved and expressing any sort of deep emotion was alien to him.

The driving lesson was initially terrifying but Victoria discovered she was a natural and soon got the hang of things. From then on she enjoyed every moment and by the time they returned to Marlborough

Street she not only knew the surrounding area more intimately, but was also totally in control of the car and eager to go out on her next drive.

She parked the car more or less next to the kerb and heaved on the handbrake. 'It's not nearly as complicated as it looks. I think after another few goes I should be quite safe to go out even when it is freezing. What do you think?'

'I think you're a quick study, darling. If you can drive, then I don't have to, which suits me just fine.' Victoria went out three more times with him beside her and then he pronounced her safe to drive solo. She experienced a new freedom; for the first time in her life she could take herself wherever she wanted and not have to rely on public transport or taxis to get there. Petrol was no longer rationed, so that was another bonus. Her new passion was exploring Boston and the surrounding countryside alone in the family car.

Towards the end of the month Taylor got a call from the gallery owner and he replaced the receiver looking somewhat bemused.

'He really likes my drawings; says they're too good for Boston. He wants to arrange a show for me in London and New York.'

'That's wonderful, darling. I've been telling you

how brilliant you are – maybe now you'll believe me. Will he want more than the drawings? Has he seen any of your new stuff yet?'

Taylor had made himself a studio in one of the spare bedrooms and had rapidly acquired all the paraphernalia necessary to become a professional artist. He had been experimenting with oil paints and watercolours as well as pen and ink and pencil. She had discovered to her dismay that she was allergic to the smell of oil paints so had not been able to go into the studio and see the works in progress.

'I've got three canvases finished, a dozen or so drawings and some smaller paintings. I thought perhaps we could drive out to New England – I'd like to capture the fall and it's at its most beautiful there.'

'I see no reason why we shouldn't. There must be guest houses or hotels we can stay in. We can take Dolores. It wouldn't be fair to take Rose, even though she's better with Taylor Junior.'

'Why do we have to take anyone? You're his mom, surely you can look after him on your own for a few days?' For a moment she didn't answer. With Amelia she had fought to have sole control of her baby, had resented every moment her daughter had spent with the nanny, but somehow with her son she was quite happy to leave him in the care of Rose or Dolores.

Was this because she hadn't really bonded with him in the way she had with Amelia? After all, she'd been so ill during the first few weeks of his life.

'Of course I could, but why don't we go completely on our own? We haven't spent any time together since you've been home. In fact, if you think about it, we've only spent a week of our lives without someone else being there.' She thought he was going to refuse. There was a tightness around his mouth as if he disapproved of her suggestion.

'Sure, if that's what you want, honey. Taylor Junior would probably hate to be moved from place to place. He's better off in his own nursery with his own things.'

She released her breath. 'And now he's beginning to shuffle about on his bottom I think he'd get very frustrated being held on my lap whilst we drove.'

The trip to view the autumn leaves was arranged. Taylor decided he would drive in spite of having protested initially at the thought, and she was relegated to the role of navigator. Unlike many women she had no difficulty map-reading and was able to direct them easily out of the city and onto one of the state highways.

Watching Taylor sketch or paint was enthralling, and she was amazed at how someone with no formal training seemed to understand intuitively how to mix paints, to apply a wash, and which brushes to use. He seemed as familiar with his tools as a man who had been painting all his life.

During those four days they spent away from Boston she came to understand she'd thrown back the lid of a Pandora's box when she'd encouraged Taylor to become an artist. He was obsessed with his work. When he was painting he focused on the canvas or the paper to the exclusion of everything else. Sometimes she'd had to go and shake his arm in order to tell him it was time to eat, or that it was getting dark, or about to rain. He seemed oblivious to the elements, to anything but his painting.

Strangely she didn't mind this, indeed preferred to be on the periphery of his life – part of it, but not the lodestone. She didn't want to be anybody's reason for living. It was sad that she didn't feel the intensity of emotion she'd experienced with Henry, for when he had died she'd felt part of her had died with him.

Although she loved Taylor, she was more pragmatic about things now. Was this what growing older meant? Distancing yourself from things – not being so intense? If it was, then she was pleased. She much preferred to live her life this way, to keep a little space between herself and her husband, and she had to admit, between herself and her son.

She adored him, would fight to the death to protect him, but didn't have the closeness she'd expected. He hadn't filled the aching void in her heart Amelia had left. She had made a dreadful mistake, and sometime soon she was going to tell Taylor everything, tell him about her parents and about the baby. Even if it meant the end of her marriage, she couldn't continue hiding her past from him for much longer.

* * *

The weeks drifted on. Taylor continued to paint furiously in his studio. The gallery owner came to see what he was doing and had been embarrassingly enthusiastic. There was talk about a Bond Street gallery in London, which would be ideal for his first one-man show. Victoria doubted if London post-war was ready to spend on an unknown artist, especially an American one.

She persuaded Taylor he would be better starting small and seeing how things went. Eventually the gallery owner, Gus Brown, agreed to hold a small exhibition of drawings, and one or two canvases and watercolours, in the New Year. If this was successful he would arrange with a gallery in New York to have a major exhibition. London wasn't mentioned again.

Christmas in America was quite different from any she'd ever known before. Santa Claus came, not Father Christmas, and everyone went wild with tinsel and glass baubles. She couldn't wait to spend her first festive season with her husband and child. She'd overspent and overdecorated. Taylor's reaction to the extravagance was typically understated. He put it down to the austerity of the war years, the time she'd spent in the Blitz, and was quite happy to go along with whatever she wanted. However, the faces of the starving she'd seen lining the streets of Calcutta kept intruding on her tinsel-filled world.

A parcel arrived from India with gifts for them all, thankfully not anything more than friends of the family would send. She'd sent a generous parcel of things that were unavailable in India; what Otis had thought of the enormous box he'd been told to mail she had no idea. Although he smiled a lot, he rarely initiated a conversation; he wouldn't bother to mention the errand to anyone, even his family.

There'd been no word from Taylor's folks, as he called them. He wasn't inclined to re-establish the relationship and she was more than happy to leave things as they were. They now attended a church in their own neighbourhood and she was beginning to make friends amongst the other young mothers. She missed the camaraderie of nursing and thought she was wasting her hard-earned skills; when things were more settled between them she was going to suggest she found herself a job at the local hospital.

* * *

Taylor's exhibition was a huge success. The private view was well attended and by the end of the evening all his work had a red dot proudly displayed in the corner.

The next morning they were sitting over a late breakfast, Taylor Junior banging his spoon noisily on his high chair making his father wince. Eventually Taylor reached out and took the spoon away from his son and the resulting tantrum brought Rose and Dolores running. 'For God's sake do something about that child, Victoria. I've got a bloody awful headache and that racket is making it worse.'

'Serves you right. You had far too much to drink last night. Give the spoon back to Taylor and he'll stop crying.'

'Here you are, noisy brat. Make as much noise as you like. I'm taking my coffee up to the studio where I can get some peace and quiet.'

Dolores handed the baby the crust from a piece of toast and he dropped the spoon, happy to munch rather than bang. 'Thank you, we should have thought of that. As you can see Taylor and I are suffering from overindulgence last night.' She got to her feet just as the wall-mounted telephone added its harsh clang to the room.

'Hi, Victoria, it's Gus here. That sure was a swell evening last night. Everything sold – WORL want to interview Taylor later today and the local press will be there as well. How is he this morning?'

'Hung-over and grumpy. But he's delighted with the sales. In fact, he's in his studio working as we speak. What time do you want him there?'

'Around two o'clock. Can he bring some of his big canvases? A couple of the seascapes and, say, three of his jungle ones?'

'I'll tell him. Thank you for all your help.'

She turned to speak to Rose. Her head spun and the last thing she remembered was the floor coming up to meet her and then nothing. She came around in bed, Taylor sitting by her side.

'You fainted, sweetheart, but you're fine now.'

Victoria stared at him. How did he know she was fine? She was well aware she'd fainted as she had the bruises to prove it, but unlike her husband she knew exactly what was wrong with her. 'I'm not fine, Taylor. I'm pregnant.'

Instead of the stunned reaction she'd expected he grinned. 'I know that, honey. I guessed a couple of weeks ago – I was waiting for you to catch on.'

'How could you possibly know that? I'm only a few weeks past my date; I'm a nurse and I wasn't even certain until I passed out just then.'

'I know your dates. It's the worst time of the month for both of us. Five long days with no sex.'

Victoria wasn't sure if she was annoyed or amused by his frank confession. 'I had a few dizzy spells last time, but not as early as this. The baby will be due in July, around the middle of the month.'

'That sure puts an end to our plans to migrate for the summer. You'll not want to be away from here at the end of your pregnancy.'

'I'm sorry, Taylor, do you mind very much not moving? We can go next year.'

He bent down and kissed her gently on the forehead. 'No, I'm thrilled. This time I shall be around to take care of you and to see my new son or daughter when he's born. I can't wait.'

'Oh, there was a phone call for you, from Gus. You have to be at the gallery for a radio and newspaper interview, and he wants a selection of your larger canvases.'

'I'll cancel it. I'm not leaving you alone this afternoon.'

'Don't be silly, darling, this could be your big opportunity. I'm going to get up in a minute and come and help you choose the pictures to take with you.'

It was late when he returned. She had put the baby to bed and eaten her supper when she heard his key in the door. 'I'm in the sitting room. If you want anything to eat, Dolores has left something in the icebox.'

He didn't answer, but she could hear him taking off his coat and draping it over the banisters. Concerned by his continued silence she scrambled up. He walked in as she reached the door. She took one look at his face and knew something was wrong.

'Taylor, what is it? What's happened? You look so strange.'

11

BETRAYAL

'Nothing's wrong, honey – in fact everything is great. Gus wants me to take my exhibition to New York; it seems I am exactly what the art world needs – a combination of war hero and raw artistic talent.' He smiled wryly as he ran his fingers through his hair.

'But that's wonderful, darling. When is the exhibition?'

'That's the problem. It's going to be in the summer sometime; it could be when the baby is due. I told him that he'd have to arrange it for August or September or I wouldn't go in person.'

Victoria wasn't sure how to react. She was pleased with his success, of course – it had been her idea that he become a professional artist – but for him to go away just before, or just after, the baby was born, to face yet another delivery without the support of her husband, surely that wasn't fair?

'What if the only slot at the gallery is in July? What will you do then?'

He shook his head. 'I don't know. I guess if push comes to shove, I'll have to go. If I'm serious about making painting my career then I've got to go to the opening of my first major one-man show. The critics and buyers will expect to meet the artist.'

She nodded; this was no more than she expected. 'Let's just pray you don't have to make that choice. But I can tell you I really don't want to go through the delivery without my husband there to support me for a second time.' She'd almost said third time but prevented herself in time.

He smiled, the long slow smile she found irresistible. 'Let's hit the sack, sweetheart.' She walked into his arms, pushing her doubts and worries to the back of her mind.

Since Taylor Junior's arrival she'd done some research into the awful depression she'd suffered after his birth and it seemed that 'baby blues' – as it was called – was a common phenomenon in postnatal women. In fact suffering as she'd done was unusual, but not unheard of. She had got off relatively lightly, but God knows what would have happened if Taylor hadn't returned when he did.

She barely remembered those black weeks, but it had affected her relationship with her son and she wasn't going to let that happen again. This time she wanted everything to be perfect. She wanted a husband at her side, wanted to come home surrounded by flowers and congratulatory cards, not an empty house and only servants for support. She frowned. Dolores and Rose were more friends than staff now and that's how she wanted it to be.

* * *

Victoria waited until she was four months gone before registering her pregnancy with her doctor. She still had the lurking fear that he would discover this was in fact not her second pregnancy, so didn't want to risk an internal examination until she was ready to deliver. The baby was due in the middle of July, the same week as Taylor's exhibition opening in a prestigious gallery in New York.

There had been no negotiation with the gallery; the exhibition would not take place unless Taylor was there in person and so he had no choice. She had been forced to accept his decision with good grace, but deep down she resented it, felt he was putting his fledgling career before his family.

As the months passed she grew larger and began to have nightmares about what might happen after her baby was born and her husband was not there to help her. Her fear coloured her every move. Taylor was oblivious to everything apart from his painting. He had to finish the last few canvases by the end of April in order for them to be packed and shipped to arrive in time to be hung. It now seemed he had to be there for the hanging, which meant he would be leaving at the beginning of July and would be gone until the third week. They both prayed that this baby, unlike Taylor Junior, would arrive late and allow his father to fly back and be there when it came.

Towards the end of May they were sitting outside in the yard, Taylor Junior toddling round their feet babbling happily to himself when Rose appeared at the back door.

'Mr King, sir, there's someone here to see you.'

Taylor looked up, irritated by the interruption. 'Well, Rose, who is it? Do I need to come or can you get rid of them?'

The young woman, now heavy with her own pregnancy, shuffled uncomfortably from foot to foot. 'I think you'd better come, sir, and see who it is yourself.'

Victoria was dozing, eyes closed, the filtered sunlight playing over her features. She waved a languid hand in her husband's direction. 'Go on, Taylor, see who it is. If you need me, I'll come, but otherwise I'm quite content to laze about out here.'

Taylor Junior saw his father leaving and set off a wail of protest. Without a second thought his father reached down, scooping the baby up to place him on his hip with practised ease. 'Come along, son, let's go and see who it is disturbing your mommy's rest.'

* * *

Taylor walked out into the hallway smiling at his son, and looked around surprised to find the vestibule empty. 'Where's my visitor, Rose?'

'She's in the drawing room, sir. I thought it better she waited in there.'

Taylor saw something – was it a warning? – flicker across the woman's face. Some instinct made him hand his baby to her. 'Here, take care of this little fellow, but don't take him outside again; his mom's sleeping.'

With a sinking feeling in his stomach he stepped

into the room to be faced by a young woman he'd hoped never to see again.

'It's taken me a long time to track you down, Taylor King, but here I am, like the proverbial bad penny, and we need to talk.'

Taylor felt his lunch threaten to return. He swallowed the bile that flooded his throat and stared at the woman. 'Anita, what the hell are you doing here?' This was all he could manage. He knew his voice sounded strained, but he was suffering from terminal shock. He'd had a brief affair with this young Englishwoman because she reminded him of his wife. It had meant nothing and he'd thought she'd understood that at the time.

'Well, why don't you offer me a seat? Ask if I'd like something to drink?'

He ignored her. The sooner he got rid of her the better. He wanted her out of the house and away before Victoria came in to investigate who his visitor was.

'I asked you a question, Anita. What are you doing here? Why have you come all this way to find me?'

She didn't answer, looked around, selected a comfortable seat and folded herself onto it, crossing her trim ankles and allowing her softly pleated cotton skirt to fall away revealing more of her long legs than she ought. 'I have something here to show you. Why don't you sit down? I think you'll need to.' She opened her handbag with a snap and removed an envelope and without further comment handed it to him. He could see there were two photographs inside.

His hands started to shake. He knew already what he was going to see. He pulled the grainy black-and-white pictures out and sure enough, staring back at him, was his own image. He'd fathered an illegitimate child with this woman.

His eyes blurred. He wanted to rip the pictures up in denial, but the face of the infant staring back at him was so familiar, he knew it was a boy. Unlike Taylor Junior, this baby was his mirror image.

'My God, how could this have happened? We used protection; were so careful.'

'Not careful enough, obviously. When I realised I was pregnant I knew I had to find you and tell you. I wanted to give you a chance to do the right thing. Then I discovered you were already married when we had our affair. You didn't think to mention that at the time, did you? You also have another son. He'd be two months older than Jack.'

'What do you want?'

'You're a wealthy man; I'm an unmarried mother.' She glanced down at the gold band on her finger with a wry smile. 'I know, as far as my family are concerned I'm a grieving widow – there are so many of us in Britain nobody has questioned it so far. However, Jack is your son too. He needs your financial support even if he can't have your physical presence.'

Taylor collapsed onto the nearest chair, dropping his head in his hands, his head spinning in disbelief. How could his life be so great one minute and was now totally fucked up? He raised his head and stared at her, his expression bleak. 'Why did you come in person? Surely you could have written, sent me photographs and got the same result?'

'I thought you should meet your son, thought it would be easier for you to make a decision, offer us financial help if you saw him face to face.'

'Meet him? Jesus Christ! Are you telling me he's here in Boston with you?' His heart raced in panic. If anyone saw her, anyone who knew him, they'd recognise the connection immediately. 'You can't stay in Boston; it's too risky. How much do you want to go away?'

The girl flinched and her eyes glistened with unshed tears. He'd said the wrong thing. This wasn't a hardened, grasping woman; this was someone no different from Victoria, who had come here in good faith to do the best for her son, his son as well. This was his mess; he'd have to sort it out somehow.

'There are some things you don't understand, Anita. This house, it's not mine – it's rented and the rent is paid by my wife. I don't have much money. I have a small income from my trust fund; everything else is my wife's. We're expecting a second baby in July. Don't you see, you being here could ruin everything for all of us?'

He saw the shock register on her face and she scrambled out of the chair, her former bravado vanished. 'My God, I'm so sorry, another baby – why didn't I think of that? I'll go, but I'm not leaving Boston until you come to see us both. I'm staying down by the station, in a small motel.' She scrabbled in her bag and handed him a card with the address and phone number scribbled on it.

'Promise me you'll come. I don't want to ruin anybody's life, but I've come all this way. I've used every last penny I had to do so, and I'm not going back until you've met your son.'

'I'll come, but not today, maybe not tomorrow, but in the next few days. Give me time to think about this; work out how I can help you both. I'm not brushing you off, Anita. I know this is as much my fault as yours. But you see how things are?' As he spoke, he gripped her by the elbow and almost bundled her out of the room, across the hall to the front door. Still hanging on, just in case she decided to run back and insist on meeting Victoria, he pulled open the door.

'All right, you don't have to throw me out. Leave me some dignity, please.' The young woman, who until she had appeared at his home he'd completely forgotten about, looked him in the eye. 'I know now I was wrong to come, to drag my baby across the world on the off chance that you... that you would wish to make a life with us. I can see now you barely remember me, but, Taylor, I loved you. I wouldn't have slept with you otherwise.'

Those were her parting words, and he stood on the doorstep and watched her walk away – tall, dark, slim, so like his darling wife he felt doubly wretched. And he couldn't get baby Jack's face out of his head.

* * *

Victoria woke from her doze wondering where her son and husband were. After yawning, stretching, and enjoying the early summer sunshine, she swung her legs to the floor and stood up. Good – her ankles had gone down. She needed the bathroom, was grateful there was a lavatory on the ground floor. She was beginning to find stairs a nuisance as she had with her previous pregnancies.

She hurried into the vestibule and across to the WC, arriving in the nick of time. Having washed her face and adjusted her clothing, she emerged to find Taylor closing the front door behind him and looking as if his world had ended.

'Taylor, who was it? What's wrong? Has someone died in your family?'

He shook his head, seemed unable to answer her. He waved a hand in her direction; she wasn't sure if it was a warning to keep away or asking for understanding, and then he turned and, taking the stairs two at a time, vanished into his studio. She heard the bolt being rammed home behind him.

She stood, marooned in the middle of the parquet floor, hardly knowing what to think or what to do. Who had come like a spectre at the feast to turn her husband from a happy man into a walking ghost? He'd gone out with Taylor Junior on his hip, so Rose must have the baby and she would know who the visitor had been. She had a dreadful feeling about all this, as if some catastrophe was about to engulf them and this time it wasn't of her making, but his.

She hurried into the kitchen where she could hear the sound of her baby babbling and laughing. She burst in, staring from one to the other and knew immediately she was about to hear something dreadful. She kissed her son, who was playing on the floor with two saucepans and a wooden spoon, and then pulled out a kitchen chair and sat down.

'Right, who's going to tell me what's going on? Who was the visitor? Why is Taylor locked in the studio and refusing to speak to me?'

The women exchanged worried glances and for a moment Victoria thought neither of them was going to tell her what she needed to know. Then Dolores came around and, pulling out the nearest chair, dropped her bulk onto the seat. She leant forward and patted Victoria's hands.

'I don't have to tell you this, ma'am, but you'll find out anyway. I reckon Mr King will tell you himself when he's sorted out what he's going to do.'

She watched the woman's face contort. Whatever it was she was going to hear it was bound to be bad.

'Dolores, I need to know – you're making it worse by dithering.'

'Well, ma'am, the visitor was a woman. I have to tell you she sure gave Rose a shock when she opened the door to her. She was so like you she could have been your sister. She asked to speak to Mr King, and wouldn't take no for an answer.'

Victoria looked at Rose. The girl's face was as pale as someone with her colouring could be and she nodded miserably. Dolores continued, her voice full of sympathy. 'Mr Taylor was shocked to see her, and they went into the drawing room, but the doors to the dining room were open and I heard every word they said. I didn't mean to eavesdrop, but once they started talking I have to admit I stayed to listen.'

The baby inside her began to kick and she placed her hands protectively over her stomach. 'Go on, Dolores. I believe I know what you're going to say, but I need to hear it from you.'

'I'm really sorry, ma'am, but the lady – Anita he called her – well, she came to find Mr King because she had a baby by him. She brought the baby over from England to meet his father. She wants him to help them financially. She didn't know he was married at the time they had the affair.' Dolores stopped and sighed loudly. 'The lady said that she loved him, and until she'd seen him and understood how it was between the two of you, she hoped he might make his life with her and their son Jack.'

Victoria sat numbly, not able to take in what she'd just been told. Taylor had had an affair in India with a woman who looked just like her while she was on her own in Boston being rejected by his parents? It didn't make sense. How could he have thrown away their marriage so casually?

He might well have spent longer with this woman than he had with her. She could forgive almost anything, but infidelity, especially when it led to the birth of an unwanted child – this was unforgivable.

In her grief and fury she forgot about her own secrets, that she had betrayed his trust; all she could think about was the man she had thought would be her partner for the rest of her life was no longer the person she wished to be with.

Like an old woman she pushed herself upright. 'I'm going out in the car with my son, Rose – you must come with me. Dolores, kindly tell Mr King I expect him to have left my house permanently by the time I return.' She choked on the last few words, but was resolute. She did not want him to leave, but didn't want to share a home with him any more.

By the time she returned to Marlborough Street, Taylor Junior was fractious and miserable from having been cooped up in the back of car with Rose for so long. She was glad to hand him over to Dolores to change his nappy and give him a long soothing drink.

'Rose, you go and lie down. I should never have asked you to come, not when you're so large. Thank you for helping me out…' Her voice trailed away as grief threatened to engulf her. She didn't need to ask if Taylor was still there; she'd known as soon as she'd set foot in the house that he'd gone.

She ran upstairs to their room. His closet was empty. The chest no longer held his neatly ironed shirts, his little balls of socks or folded boxer shorts. She sunk onto the bed and for the first time understood the enormity of her actions.

During the long day she'd driven about, stopping frequently to let her son toddle around in the sunshine, eat an ice cream or have a drink. At no time did she and Rose discuss what had happened. Victoria had focused on the matter in hand, ignoring the black hole that loomed in front of her, threatening to submerge her if she stepped off the edge of sanity.

She had condemned herself to face the rest of her life alone, bring up two children by herself, never again feel the warmth of a man's love as they lay in the hot, damp darkness. She felt too tired, too drained, to think any further than that. She swung her legs up onto the bed, noticing with clinical disinterest they were badly swollen, not a good sign at her stage of pregnancy.

She should go down and question Dolores, hear what her husband had said when he had been given her ultimatum second-hand. But right now she was too tired; she had to put her health and that of the unborn child ahead of her curiosity, even ahead of her son.

Spread out like a starfish on the bed, knowing it would seem too big for her now, she wondered if it might be better if she moved into one of the smaller spare bedrooms, which had single beds. This was all her damaged mind could cope with.

She wasn't sure how long she lay there. She might have dozed off, but she heard the voice of her son calling, 'Momma, Momma, Momma,' and her heart twisted with love for him.

She sat up and called out, 'I'm awake. Please bring Taylor Junior in here. I had to stay put as my ankles are so swollen and I needed to keep them elevated.'

Dolores appeared at the door the wriggling toddler in her arms. He was kicking and fighting to get down, to use his new expertise to travel to his mother.

She slid down so her back was resting against the side of the bed then stretched out her legs, letting the bulge of her belly settle more comfortably onto her thighs. She held out her arms.

'Come to Mommy then, darling. Come and give Mommy a big kiss.' The little boy beamed and chuckled as he tottered across the carpet, making walking look a difficult task. He flung himself the last foot and she snatched him up, holding him to her face, kissing him and blowing bubbles against his neck whilst he screamed with joy.

Over his head she met Dolores's gaze. There was no need for words; that one look said it all. She knew that her husband had gone and that he had left in such a way her friend thought the rift was permanent.

12

FRIENDSHIP

Victoria was determined to keep life as normal as possible. She refused to allow herself to think about contacting Taylor; he'd gone, and that was that. Neither was she going to sink into a deep depression; she had her unborn child and Taylor Junior to think about.

'Dolores, I'm going to stroll down to the park whilst it's still comparatively cool.'

'Yes, ma'am. Do you want me to come with you?'

'No, thank you, I shall be fine. I just need to get out of the house for a bit.' Without Taylor it no longer felt like home.

She found a shady spot and unstrapped her toddler and put him down on the grass to play with the ball and bricks she'd brought with her. The baby was content for a bit, but then demanded she sit down and join in his game. She was able to lose herself for a while in his game and could ignore her pain and misery.

'Come along, darling, it's time to go home and have your nap.' He had been rubbing his eyes and yawning so he would be happy to go. When she got back she saw her car parked outside the front door, engine running and the doors open. She increased her pace, guessing what was happening. Rose had gone into labour. Her baby wasn't due for another two weeks, but after the shock of yesterday and being bounced about in the car all day she wasn't surprised it had decided to come early.

Bumping the stroller up the front steps was difficult, but she could hardly ask for assistance. She met Otis coming down, his arm around his wife's waist, a broad grin on his face, his mother-in-law close behind.

'Rose's waters went, ma'am. They're off to the hospital. I'll stay here to take care of things for you.'

'Dolores, you must go with Rose and Otis. I'm perfectly capable of looking after myself and my son until your first grandchild is safely delivered.'

Dolores smiled. 'If you're sure, ma'am, I'd like to

go with them. There's plenty of food in the icebox, and Taylor Junior's lunch is in there too.'

Victoria looked down and saw her son was almost asleep. She unbuckled his restraining straps, carried him upstairs and put him in his cot. He didn't need the cover on. She stepped away to close the shutters, and then drew the curtains across the window, making the room cool and dark.

She looked down at her baby. He'd only just celebrated his first birthday and had already lost his father. She thought he looked vulnerable in the huge cot. Leaving the door open so she could hear him when he woke, she began her slow progress down the stairs, having to lean heavily on the banister in order to keep upright. Although there was still two months before her baby was due for some reason this time it felt as if the baby was squashing her lungs, making it difficult to breathe, difficult to walk comfortably.

She reached the hall, pausing to decide whether to go and sit in the backyard or waddle into the kitchen and get herself a snack. As she stood catching her breath, there was a hesitant bang on the brass knocker.

She smiled. Otis must have come back because they'd forgotten something. She opened the door to find a woman, a total stranger, holding a baby that looked achingly familiar. The two women stared at each other in silence. Victoria's hand was reaching out to slam the door in her face when she saw how pale the woman was, how limp and listless the child.

'You must be Anita, and that's Jack, my husband's other son. I think you'd better come in.'

The woman didn't move, as if too stunned by the invitation to take the first step. Victoria reached out and took the baby from her arms, then holding him balanced against her bump, she walked across the hall and down the passageway into the kitchen. Anita followed her, her court shoes tapping noisily on the parquet floor.

Her medical training took over. Grabbing a thick tablecloth from a drawer she spread it on the table. Putting the child on it she gave him a quick examination. She could see at once he was ill, that he had a high fever. Quickly she undid his rompers to check for the tell-tale blotches that would indicate he had meningitis. She breathed a sigh of relief. Next she ran her fingers under his chin, checking to see if his glands were raised – they were, but not dramatically. The baby began to whimper again and his eyes opened. She stared back into a pair of blue-grey eyes identical to his father's.

'He's been like this since yesterday. I can't get him

to feed. He falls asleep then wakes up and cries. I have no money to take him to a doctor, and the people at the motel told me to take him out as he was disturbing the other guests. I've nowhere else to go. I'm so sorry, I shouldn't have come here, but I was desperate.'

Victoria looked up and seeing the desolation on a face that could belong to a member of her own family, she smiled. 'It doesn't matter now. I threw Taylor out when I found out about you and Jack; he's not here any more. This is between us; it's nothing to do with him. Your baby is my son's half-brother. I suppose that makes us family of a sort.'

She saw a little colour return to Anita's face and the woman almost smiled. 'If you say so. I don't understand why you're being so kind to me. I decided I hated you and your child for being the ones Taylor loves. He said he was coming to see me but I knew he wouldn't.'

'I would prefer it if you didn't talk about him. Let's concentrate on little Jack here. He doesn't need to go to hospital; he has a fever and is dehydrated. I'm a nurse. I'm quite capable of taking care of him.'

She put them in the spare room. They dragged out a large drawer from an old-fashioned chest for him to sleep in and placed it on top of the single bed to make it more accessible. With folded blankets on the base it was perfectly adequate, if a trifle Victorian.

They worked well together, and when Taylor stood up in his cot, rattling the bars and demanding to be picked up, she sent her guest in to get him and for some reason her son didn't protest at being collected by a total stranger. Anita changed him and was about to bring him into her while she was sponging down the fractious baby.

'Don't come in here with him, please. Whatever your son's got could be infectious. He's already responding. His temperature is lower than an hour ago. And he's drunk plenty of boiled water so I think there's not really anything to worry about here.'

'Shall I go down and give Taylor Junior his lunch? I could make us both a sandwich. I know my way around a kitchen. I went to catering college.'

'That's a stroke of luck, because I'm totally useless domestically. Yes, please do. I should be finished in about fifteen minutes and then I'll leave him to sleep. This room is directly above the kitchen so we'll hear him if he cries.'

Leaving the baby comfortable, she headed downstairs. She was certain the child was too poorly to attempt to scramble out of his makeshift cot, but just in case, she'd surrounded the bed with pillows and blankets.

Her son was burbling and gurgling whilst banging his spoon on the tray of his highchair. Victoria went towards the noise, not quite knowing how to deal with this strange situation. Like Anita, she'd been prepared to hate the woman who'd ruined her life, but having met her, and her baby, she realised the blame lay with Taylor and it was he they should both turn their anger on, not each other.

'He's asleep. I'm pretty sure it's just one of those bugs babies get. He'll wake up tomorrow hungry and almost back to normal.'

Automatically she walked over and kissed her son who grinned up at her but continued banging and shouting in rhythm, 'Momma – Momma – Momma.'

'I thought that's what he was saying. He's very young to be talking. How old is he?'

'He was one last month. He says quite a few words now, but mostly Momma and Dada.'

Her words hung between them – the air was thick with tension. What was she doing, sharing a house with someone who had, however inadvertently, been the cause of making her son and unborn baby fatherless?

She turned away and removed the cloth she had

laid Jack on from the table and took it into the laundry room in order to give herself time to think. When she came back Anita was sitting at the table her head dropped onto her arms, her shoulders shaking.

All this was far worse for Jack and his unmarried mother. She had no protection in law, no money, was alone in a strange country with a sick baby. She put her arm around the woman's shoulders.

'Please don't cry. We both have to get used to... well get used to not having Taylor. I don't blame you, I know you thought he was single and... well let's forget about how all this started and concentrate on the present, shall we?'

She pulled open a drawer and removed a napkin to hand to the sobbing woman. It would have to do; she wasn't going upstairs again to fetch a clean handkerchief. Eventually Anita sat back, drying her eyes and sniffing loudly.

'I don't deserve your kindness, or support. I knew before I came to America Taylor was married, that he had a child, but I still came with the intention... I think with the intention of stealing him from you. I'm a horrible person. I shouldn't be here, and you shouldn't be looking after us.' Her voice trailed off and Victoria feared she was going to succumb to another bout of sobbing.

'Dry your eyes,' she said briskly. 'Enough of this, Anita. I've told you, you must forget about how you come to be here, about everything apart from what's going on at the moment. You're safe, your son's upstairs, I'm here to help. I'm seven months pregnant admittedly – but I still think we can get through this together.'

'And don't forget your son's here, banging his tray and demanding his lunch.' Anita stood up and, going to the cooker, tipped the bowl of previously prepared gunk that had been warming over a pan of hot water into a cold dish and handed it to Victoria. 'This is ready; if you feed him I'll make us something to eat.'

'Okay, thanks. My ankles are swelling a lot more this time and I need to stay off my feet as much as possible.' After hooking a chair round, she sat down and began the ritual of spooning food into her son. Luckily, he was a good eater and she had no need to play aeroplanes or birds in order to get him to eat. He gobbled it down and by the time he'd finished Anita was placing a steaming mug of coffee, a jug of cream, bowl of sugar and two rounds of beautifully manicured sandwiches, in front of her.

'Heavens, you cut the crusts off? What luxury. Could you fetch him a banana from the fruit bowl and give him a couple of pieces?'

Whilst clutching a chunk of banana in each hand Taylor Junior was content. Victoria was sitting opposite Anita and prepared to enjoy her lunch. However, Anita took a few mouthfuls and then put her sandwich down.

'I'm just going to pop up and see how Jack is. I know we can hear him, but I just want to be sure he hasn't woken up and tried to escape.'

Victoria watched her go. There was so much she didn't know about this woman; in fact, she knew little apart from her name. She'd met Taylor somewhere in Burma and she was a cook. A chef? An unusual occupation for a woman, but then during the war women had been driving buses, trains and ambulances, so being a chef in the army was probably quite normal. She continued to eat her sandwich finding, in spite of everything, she was hungry.

'Jack's fast asleep, and he's much cooler and less flushed. I think I must have panicked rather, don't you?'

'I'm hardly surprised – with what's been happening to you these past few days. I think I would have done the same.'

Anita shook her head. 'No, you wouldn't, you're a much stronger person than me. I would never have invited you into my house and taken care of you if the situation had been reversed. But I wouldn't have had the strength to send Taylor packing either.'

She looked at her in surprise. A strong woman? When had this metamorphosis taken place? She'd always believed she was a weak person, someone who had given in to depression and allowed the blackness to overwhelm her – not once, but twice. But she wasn't going to tell Anita that. She rather liked the praise even if it was undeserved.

'Do you have a return ticket?'

'Yes, I do. I sailed over on the *Queen Elizabeth*, tourist, but it was quite comfortable; a lot better than the troopship I went to India in, I can tell you.'

This was the opportunity she needed to enquire more about her visitor's past. 'I was going to ask you how you came to be in India. I think I've already told you I was a member of the Queen Alexandra's. How did you get out there?'

'I joined the Catering Corps. I didn't have the stomach for nursing or the aptitude, but I've always been good with food. My parents run a country pub and I could cook almost before I could read and write. As I said earlier, my parents paid for me to go to college so when the war broke out I automatically chose catering. Very soon I was promoted and I volunteered for overseas duty and found myself eventually in India, organising the officers' mess, and later on, at the front.'

She had to ask. 'How did you meet Taylor?'

The girl blushed and shifted in her seat. 'I thought we were going to leave this in the past?'

Victoria knew Taylor must have made the first move. How could he have done that so soon after they were married? 'You're right, India is taboo. I've been here since last November and I hate it. I've decided to go back to England and I have a proposition for you.'

She didn't know where these ideas were coming from, but whilst listening to Anita she'd felt a connection with this woman that went beyond Taylor – the same feeling she'd had with Molly, the girl she had met when she first joined up and who had been savagely murdered whilst they were nursing in Africa.

'I think you know that I'm independently wealthy. Taylor has some money, but not much, so he's not in a position to support you and Jack, but I am. I know it's bizarre, but I feel we could be really good friends in spite of the way we met. And Jack and Taylor Junior are brothers; it's right they should grow up together, however strange the circumstances.'

She stopped to marshal her thoughts. 'Something preposterous has occurred to me and I just have to tell you. I'm going to suggest that you let me adopt your son. Taylor Junior and Jack can grow up as twins. Although they are two months apart in age, they are similar in size – I don't think anyone will question it.'

Anita frowned. 'Let me get this straight, Victoria, you want to raise Jack as your own? Where does that leave me? I'm his mother. If I'd wanted to give him up I could have done so when he was born and saved myself a lot of trouble.'

'I'm not suggesting you do that. I'm only working this out as I speak. I don't mean I actually adopt him – he'll always be your child – but he should take Taylor's name. That's his right anyway, isn't it? This will make things so much easier for him at school; in fact everywhere. I was going to suggest that you become, I don't know – my companion, my housekeeper, my whatever.

'I'll pay you a salary and when I go back to nursing you will be here to take of all three children.' Victoria paused. Where had that come from? She hadn't even considered going back until the words had come out of her mouth. With more confidence, she continued. 'I have to take the exams to become a sister; I have the experience and necessary knowledge to do so. Next year I want to go back to work. I'm a good nurse and don't want to waste my expertise. I'll need someone to run the house and look after the children whilst I'm working.'

Anita's face relaxed as she understood where this convoluted conversation was leading. 'I begin to see what you're getting at now. Together we can do things that we could never do on our own. As I told you, I'm a good cook and like children. Do you know, however mad this seems, I accept your offer.'

Victoria smiled at her new friend. 'Good – that's settled. The first thing I want you to do is fetch your belongings from the motel – take a cab. Your ticket should have the telephone numbers we need to book our crossing. I'll transfer you to first class and we'll need a suite of rooms.'

She was silent, thinking hard; she probably had six weeks in which it would still be safe to travel without the risk of her baby being delivered. 'We need to leave next week. If you can organise that for us, then I'll start the financial side of things. I have to visit the bank and close my account, get the money transferred back to the bank who dealt with everything in England.'

'I can do that, but where are we going to live? Do you have a house in England as well?'

Victoria flopped back. 'God – how stupid! I hadn't thought as far as that. Have you any ideas? I think I need to be in London somewhere, but a good part of London, where there are schools and parks and not too much bomb damage if that's possible.'

'I don't know much about London, but I went to Regent's Park once, before the war. It's lovely round there, very smart and large semi-detached houses. I don't think many bombs were dropped in that part of London; it was mostly the East End.'

'Regent's Park? Yes, I think you're right. I seem to remember someone telling me RAF training took place at Lord's Cricket Ground near there. I always thought that a strange place to train pilots, but it must have been safe or they wouldn't have chosen it. It's in St John's Wood. I don't know much about the area, but if it's near the park and a cricket ground and I believe there's a zoo as well, it will be perfect for bringing up our family.'

She received a phone call from Dolores to say Rose had produced a fine, nine-pound girl; she and Otis were going to stay with the family for the next couple of nights in order to be close to them both.

That solved one problem. She didn't want to discuss her plans with Dolores until she had them finalised. This would give her a clear two days to hand in the notice on the house, close her bank account and arrange everything for the journey. They would have to stay in a hotel until they found somewhere suitable to live.

She hadn't had the strength to go into Taylor's studio; the door was closed and she'd left it that way. She didn't want to be reminded of what might have been. She could cope if she pretended nothing had happened. She felt as if, just behind her, there was a black cloud waiting to overwhelm her if she looked over her shoulder even for a second.

The next two days were spent in frantic arrangements. She decided to give her car, and all the other bits and pieces she'd accumulated over the past two years, to Dolores and her family. They could sell them or keep them; it was up to them. They would also be able to live rent-free for the next three months. She had withdrawn a large quantity of money and was going to give it to them as a parting gift; she didn't want them to refuse, so thought she would leave it in an envelope in the studio.

She was going to ask Dolores and Otis to clear and clean the house and leave it pristine for the next tenants. She would be sad to say goodbye to them but knew she'd made the right decision. On the third day after the upheaval she got up to find Taylor – she no longer called him Junior as he was now the only one with that name – wasn't in his cot. She checked across the corridor and saw that Jack and Anita were also up.

She looked at her wristwatch, amazed to see it was after nine o'clock. This was the best sleep she'd had in months; she was refreshed, invigorated, ready to cope with anything. Today she would go into the studio, leave the envelope in a prominent place and say her final goodbyes to Taylor and her life in America.

She braced herself and walked in to find he'd left just one easel and standing on it was a self-portrait. He'd captured his long Bostonian features, streaky brown hair and blue-grey eyes perfectly. He had the slightly whimsical smile playing on his lips that she would always associate with the toe-curling preliminaries to lovemaking.

Clipped to the watercolour was an envelope with her name on. She forced herself to walk over and take it, pulling out a sheet of paper. She noticed there was a second sheet inside but ignored that. She scanned the contents with dismay. Taylor had written that he would wait to hear from her for forty-eight hours and if she didn't contact him by then he'd know their marriage was truly over, that she'd meant what she said.

In which case he was leaving for New York, to start a new life and wouldn't contact her again. She thought she would faint. She bit hard on her lips and tasted blood. That steadied her. She removed the portrait and pushed his paper back in the envelope not bothering to read the second sheet. She dropped the envelope of money in its place.

It was done. It was over. Fate had taken a hand in things and not left her to make a difficult decision. She closed her eyes and prayed, hoping God would look kindly on Taylor in spite of his weaknesses. She wished him good luck in his new career and hoped one day they might meet again when all this was behind them and that he would find a place in his life for his children.

PART III

LONDON, 1947–49

13

ADOPTING JACK

Victoria gazed out of the kitchen window into the garden of the house she'd bought in Ellis Gardens, a smart cul-de-sac within bowling distance of Lord's Cricket Ground and no more than a mile from Regent's Park. She could hear her children playing. Anita was laughing as she sprayed them with water from the hosepipe.

It hardly seemed possible she had been in England over a year. Lydia had been born at the end of July and was now a sturdy fourteen months. She was adored by her older brothers and in return she followed them about, desperately trying to emulate their every move. She was a hybrid of the two, having her dark hair and Taylor's strange blue-grey eyes.

The builders were banging about next door converting the adjoining property for her. They had promised the alterations would be completed before Christmas and then she would finally have the house she wanted. The semi-detached, stucco-faced Victorian villa she'd bought in St John's Wood had three large bedrooms, a box room and a bathroom plus a spacious loft upstairs; a long living room stretching the width of the house, dining room, downstairs lavatory and big kitchen-cum-breakfast room at the back. The small porch led directly into a square hall from which the stairs led up to the bedrooms. This central corridor cut the house in two – running from the front to the back.

It had a pretty front garden with a low brick wall and high laurel hedge. French doors opened from the sitting room onto a brick terrace. The garden was divided into lawn with a few trees and flower beds down either side, and a large vegetable plot.

It wasn't big enough for her growing family, hence the purchase of the adjoining property. The children were sharing one of the bedrooms at the moment, which meant Lydia would have had to have the box room if she didn't enlarge the house. In two months' time the decorators could move in and then she would have a much-needed extra bathroom with a separate shower cubicle. She missed being able to have a shower every day, and there would be more than enough bedrooms for all of them.

The house next door had had a garage added and this, plus the sitting room, was being converted into a small, self-contained flat. The extra kitchen and dining room would be incorporated into their downstairs living accommodation. She would then have a study and the other room could be a playroom or extra sitting room.

Taylor – who was now called Junior as it had been too hard hearing the name Taylor all the time – came racing up to the window dripping with water.

'Mummy we're really, really hungry. Can we have tea out here? Please, please, can we?'

'Of course you can. Ask Anita to dry you. I'll start bringing the trays; it's all ready.'

Her son ran off telling the others the good news. She heard Jack shouting and squeals of delight from Lydia, who would not have understood the message but always joined in with any shouting. Jack was so like Taylor it was almost painful to see him grinning back at her over the table every day.

She thought a lot about her husband, had sent a

card announcing Lydia's birth to Gus, who was now his agent, and received a polite letter of congratulations, which could have been from a total stranger. The huge cheque enclosed, Taylor said, was to contribute towards his children's upbringing. It had done more than that; it had paid for the house next door.

Anita appeared at the kitchen door shaking water from her hair. 'I forgot to tell you, Victoria, I've been asked to work this weekend. Is that okay?'

'No problem. I'm not on the roster again until the end of the month.'

'Yes, of course, you told me that yesterday.'

* * *

They shared the ritual of putting the children to bed as they always did when they were both home. Victoria, for the umpteenth time, wondered how Anita coped with hearing her son calling another woman mummy. They did talk about it sometimes, but Anita shrugged, saying you did what you had to when your children's well-being was at stake.

The flat next door was so Victoria could employ live-in staff and she had found a couple, Bert and Ada Thompson, who already came in on a daily basis to do the general cleaning and help out wherever needed. Bert looked after the massive, solid fuel boiler and took care of the garden and any handiwork. At the moment they were living in a damp basement flat and had been overjoyed to accept her offer of free accommodation as soon as it was ready.

They should be in by Christmas and then Anita would be free to take on more shifts at the hotel in Maida Vale where she'd found herself a job. They'd soon realised neither of them wanted to be at home all day. Anita loved the children, but was not as maternal as she'd expected; in fact Victoria found she was more content to stay at home with the three of them than her friend. The occasional shifts she did at a local hospital were sufficient to satisfy her need to use her nursing expertise and allow her to mix with other professionals.

A week later the two women were eating their evening meal in companionable silence. They were good friends – in fact more like sisters – and the only thing they never discussed was the father of their children.

Anita replaced her cutlery quietly and looked up, her face troubled. 'There's something I've got to tell you, Victoria... I've met someone, and I think... well I'm certain he's the one for me.'

She felt sick. 'Does this mean you're leaving, taking Jack away?'

'No, that's the point. I told Frank I'd had an illegitimate child, but I told him he was adopted. He doesn't know I'm still in contact with my son. He thinks I'm a completely free agent. He's quite a bit older than me; he comes from Yorkshire and owns several factories up there. I met him a few months ago when he was in London on business; he has been coming back more and more often and last time he asked me to marry him.'

'Good grief! And you never told me anything? How could you keep something like this to yourself, Anita? I thought we were honest with each other, that we talked about everything.'

She was shocked, and deeply hurt by this revelation, but overjoyed Jack would become her sole responsibility, that she would no longer have to share his affection with his real mother. He felt like her son. She loved him as much as she did her other two children, as much she did her missing daughter, Amelia.

'I didn't tell you because we agreed not to talk about Taylor and I thought Frank came into that category. Also, the reason I've been working night shifts and weekends... well... some of those times – in fact I wasn't working at all, I was out with him.'

'I see. When are you planning to get married?'

'There are some things we need to get sorted out before we do that. I want you to adopt Jack legally, then I can leave him with you knowing he'll have a wonderful life growing up with his brother and sister. I think that might take a few weeks and I thought I'd wait until Bert and Ada are in residence. I'm not going to leave you in the lurch.'

'How very considerate of you.' She'd allowed her disappointment to show and regretted her sarcasm. 'I'm sorry, I didn't mean that. I'm really happy for you – you deserve to find love again.' She jumped up and ran around the table to embrace her friend. They were both tearful when she stepped back.

'The builders told me they'll be ready to knock through next week, then they just need to connect all the plumbing and the radiators and things to our new boiler and the carpenters and decorators can get started. They promised me faithfully they'll be gone before Christmas.'

'Well, it's the middle of September now, so that gives them three months. I'll stay for Christmas, and then leave in the New Year. I'll tell Frank he can set the date for the beginning of January.'

'I suppose I can't come to your wedding or meet your husband?'

Anita shook her head. 'I don't think you'd better. I don't want him to know anything about us. I hope you understand. It's just that... well I want to make a fresh start, and the only way I can do it is if I cut you and the children out of my life completely. It's going to tear me apart, but I have no choice.'

'I understand – I know all about having to give things up.' She almost told Anita her secrets, but restrained the impulse. When she finally spoke about Amelia it would be to her parents.

* * *

The builders, knowing there was a generous bonus waiting if they completed their work ahead of schedule, got things done by the beginning of December and the Thompsons were there to celebrate Christmas with them. The decorations were still up, Christmas tree twinkling with little electric fairy lights, when Anita left the house for the last time.

'I'm going to make this brief. I've written a long letter for Jack. Can you give it to him when you think he's old enough to read it?' They'd agreed they would tell the children about Jack's parentage at some point, when they were old enough to understand. Fortunately, the adoption had been surprisingly easy to arrange, and she was now Jack's mother, the mother of four children not three. She blinked back unwanted tears as she thought of her missing child.

Anita turned and ran down the front path and out to the waiting black taxicab. She'd timed her departure for the evening, when all three children were asleep. She couldn't bring herself to say goodbye to them as well.

Victoria closed the door behind her friend for the last time and pushed home the bolts. She would miss Anita, would miss her dreadfully. They'd become very close over the past eighteen months, but for some reason her spirits lightened – it was as if a weight had been lifted from her shoulders.

Why was this? Perhaps it was because Jack would never be taken away from her, that he was now legally her son, or maybe the fact her parents were coming to stay in the spring was the reason. Instead of feeling devastated by Anita's departure, she actually felt liberated.

* * *

At the start of New Year, 1948, post-war Britain was more miserable than it had been during the war. The new Labour government had introduced the National

Health Service and so for the first time ordinary people could see a doctor and not worry about the cost. The damage from the Blitz and by the V1 and V2 rockets was so extensive in some parts of East London that it might be years before things were rebuilt and life was back to normal. The poor men returning from fighting for their country, like their compatriots after the First World War, didn't return to a wonderful new life at all.

They found that their womenfolk had become independent and were reluctant to give up jobs they'd been doing so efficiently over the past six years. Children returned from evacuation and in many cases no longer felt any affinity with their actual families. Rationing was as stringent, and after the plenty of America she had found it difficult to adjust to having to make do and mend still.

Fortunately, Bert had grown an abundance of vegetables; he had the proverbial green fingers. He'd grown enough to keep the family over the winter. Ada, used to queuing for things, was quite happy to continue to do so when necessary. However, as she made all their bread – having relations in the country who sent up bags of flour – that was one staple they didn't have to do without.

Victoria was still in contact with Dolores and her

family and looked forward to receiving their letters. They'd used the money she'd given them to start a business: a small general store and deli on the north side of Boston, amongst their family and friends. They sent regular food parcels, which meant the children didn't have to rely on their meagre sweet ration. The Hershey bars and tinned fruit supplied regular treats – in fact they were all very lucky.

That morning she had received a letter from her parents. Her mother was her most frequent correspondent, but her father usually added a page or two in his tiny black scrawl. Independence in India had not turned out to be the universal panacea everyone had expected. Millions of people had died in the partition. Muslims had been forced to trek the length of India in order to live in the new Pakistan, and Hindus had had to leave the north and move down into new India. This was when the religious killing had taken place.

Her father had suffered a mild heart attack and, although he was fully recovered, he'd immediately resigned his position in the government, finding everything far too stressful. It was now more than three years since Victoria had met them in Madras – far too long. She'd told them all about Jack and they thought of him as one of their own grandchildren.

Victoria had also removed herself from the relief roster at the hospital. She didn't feel she could be away from the children at the moment, not when Anita wasn't there. Ada was wonderful and the children loved her, but Anita had been their second mother and they didn't understand why she had abandoned them.

That night Victoria lay in her large bed and her thoughts turned to Taylor, something she had denied herself for many years. Anita's departure, and marriage, had finally given her permission to think about her husband. It would have been disloyal whilst her friend was there, and he certainly couldn't come back to live in a *ménage à trois*. Anita had left of her own volition, so now was the time to contact him and ask him to come and visit his children.

Every quarter she received a massive cheque from Taylor; these were banked in a savings account to pay for the children's education. She had no idea where he was getting the money, but assumed his career as a professional artist had taken off and he was being paid vast sums for his canvases. She wasn't really surprised – he was a talented artist.

She had no idea where he was, in New York somewhere she supposed. The money came from his lawyers in Boston and didn't contain a forwarding address. She had forgiven his infidelity a long time ago. How could she do anything else when his weakness had given her Jack? She'd been forced to accept he was not the perfect husband, he was selfish and weak, but she still loved him despite his many failings.

Were his failings because he was a man? Did all men behave like this? She didn't have much experience, apart from Henry and Taylor. The men she'd worked with during the war had all been professionals – they put their job first, as she had, and she had no idea what they were like in their private lives.

Women might be revered, put on pedestals, but they were also expected to remain in the background, be homemakers and not show any independence or dissent. The war had changed a lot of this; for women who had held responsible jobs were no longer willing to remain second-class citizens in their own county. Eventually attitudes would change and women would be treated equally. Those who chose to work would not be regarded as freaks and unfeminine. She sighed. This was just a pipe dream, but she prayed by the time her daughters were adults their horizons would be wider.

Her parents were arriving on April 7th and this gave her several months to decide whether to contact Taylor. Whatever the outcome of this proposed meeting their relationship would never be the same – he would have to accept she was independent – quite capable of running a house and raising their children without his assistance. If he wanted to be a part of their lives it would have to be on her terms this time.

14

INDIAN OR ENGLISH?

The front garden was bursting with spring flowers. Late daffodils, tulips and hyacinths bloomed between wallflowers and forget-me-nots. Victoria thought her parents would be impressed. This was the warmest April anyone could remember, more like June really.

When the dividing wall between the two properties had been removed Bert had dug an island bed in the space and planted rose bushes and these appeared to be about to burst into flower. They were covered with shining red-green leaves and bulging buds and promised to look stunning this summer.

Her two boys were searching for stray pieces of litter that might have blown in from the pavement that ran alongside the wall, but as they lived in a cul-de-sac they were going to be unlucky.

'Junior, Jack, I don't think there's any to be found. You've already picked up all the sticks and stones – that's enough for now. Grandpa and Grandma are bound to notice the beautiful job you've done tidying the front garden.' She could hear her daughter inside with Ada, happily stirring a cake mix.

'These flowers smell nice, Mummy. Can I pick some?'

'You'd better not, Jack. Bert will shoot you.' The little boy laughed and stepped back. He understood how much Bert loved his flowers.

'Mummy, you've told us that Grandpa is Indian and Grandma is English, so are you Indian or English?'

'That's a good question, Junior. A mixture of both, like you are all half American and a quarter English and a quarter Indian.' She hated lying to Jack, but had no choice.

The boys frowned, not exactly sure what a quarter was. She laughed at them. 'Don't worry about it, darlings – what you need to know is that you've got American blood from your father, and Indian and English from me, so you're a jolly good mix.'

It bothered her that Junior held dual nationality.

As he had been born in America, he was an American, subject to their call-up rules and so on. Jack and Lydia had been born in England so, although they had an American father, they were English on their passports. Well, they would be if they had one of their own.

'Come along, let's go in and check everything's ready. They should be here very soon now.'

The two boys ran in, jostling and pushing to be the first through the open front door. Their rivalry was intense but friendly, thank goodness. She followed, smiling as her sons rushed from room to room. The flowers from the back garden were prominently displayed, as were their cards of welcome. She went to the door and watched them plumping up the pillows like a pair of miniature cleaning ladies.

Junior was slightly taller and still had floppy black hair, dark skin and her own brown eyes, but his features were like his father's; Jack, on the other hand looked exactly like Taylor but he seemed to have his mother's energy and his streaky fair hair was showing a tendency to curl like Anita's had. No one would mistake them for anything but brothers, and everyone automatically assumed they were fraternal twins, which was exactly what she wanted.

'Everything looks lovely, boys. Shall we go in the

kitchen and see if we can help with anything?' Dressed identically in cotton shorts and short-sleeved shirts they looked smart and heartbreakingly English. It was a shame they hadn't needed to don the matching pullovers Ada had knitted for them.

In the kitchen everything was running as smoothly as it always did. Lydia looked up, her face sticky with cake mix. 'Yum yum. Liddy's been licking spoons, Mummy.'

The boys instantly pulled up chairs, hoping to be given a similar treat. Ada beamed. 'Here you are, I saved you a spoon each, but don't muck up your clean clothes.' They nodded simultaneously and held out their hands.

'I'm going to check upstairs one more time.' Her children would be on their best behaviour this afternoon. They were as eager to meet their grandparents as she was. She ran upstairs and into the two bedrooms and dressing room allocated to her mother and father. Mama had assured her she was quite capable of looking after both of them, and she had to believe this was the case. She rather thought things had changed for her parents since they'd left the principality of Marpur to live in Delhi.

The violence, the massacring of columns of the Sikh refugees whose lands had been divided by the artificial border created between India and the new Pakistan, had started in Calcutta and then spread. She knew it had deeply affected both her parents, and that they were looking forward to spending several peaceful months in England away from the turmoil of their own country.

She was upstairs when she saw the taxi draw up outside. At last – after more than three long years – they were here. She could hardly believe they had come so far; this was the first time she could welcome them into her own home. She wondered how her autocratic father would adjust to being a guest in his daughter's house. She called to her children as she raced down the stairs.

'They're here. Wash your faces and hands and come with me to meet them.'

Chairs scraped back and a clamour of excited childish voices reverberated up the stairs, then Jack and Junior, Lydia between them, scampered into the hall.

'Shall Grandpa be wearing a crown?'

'Don't be stupid, Jack – he'll have a turban with great big jewels on.'

She had no idea how her father would present himself; he could be in a smart suit or his usual garb of high-necked black jacket and trousers. Her mother, the last time she had seen her, had been wearing a sari and had her fading blonde hair in a neat plait falling down her back. Would she be in Indian costume or have reverted to her European garb?

She glanced down at her own clothes; she was wearing her usual smart linen slacks, silk blouse with a round collar and flat, matching kid shoes. She had grown her hair and wore it swept up in a loose knot on top of her head. She had a slick of red lipstick and a brush of face powder, plus a generous spray of expensive French perfume. She looked just like all the other women who lived in the close.

She took the children into the garden; they waited on the front step for the taxi to disgorge its passengers. Victoria ran to open the gate, telling her children to remain where they were for the moment. She came face to face with her father; she hardly recognised him. His hair was no longer black but silver, his face thinner, and he was dressed in a smart business suit.

'My darling girl, you look absolutely wonderful.' He opened his arms, which in itself was a novelty, and she rushed forward to hug him, shocked by how insubstantial he felt. He had never been a well-built man, but now he seemed to have shrunk.

'I can't believe you're here, standing outside *my* home in St John's Wood. I am so pleased to see you both and there are three others waiting in the garden who are equally excited.'

He smiled at her. 'Then I shall go at once to introduce myself. I shall leave you to assist your mother.' Victoria's stomach lurched. Was her mother unwell? She looked round to see her mother stepping nimbly from the taxi. She had also reverted to European clothes and was dressed in the height of fashion, her hair swept up in an elegant chignon, face discreetly made-up, and she looked younger and fitter than when they'd last met in Madras; a sharp contrast to her father's appearance.

'I'm so pleased to see you.' She rushed forward, not needing to wait for permission to kiss her mother. The surly taxi driver appeared and dumped four large leather cases on the pavement.

'That'll be two pound two shillings.' Victoria had the money ready and handed him the exact amount, knowing the fare had already been increased substantially. She smiled serenely at the taxi driver.

'Thank you, is that all the luggage?' The man looked at the money – for a moment she thought he was going to say something impolite. Then to her astonishment he grinned, revealing a large space at the front of his mouth.

'That's the lot, missus. You've already given me a generous tip, thanks.'

She heard him chuckling as he got back into his taxi. Behind the high laurel hedge, she could hear her children talking eagerly to her father, his deep, clipped English voice replying. Her mother turned, keen to meet her grandchildren, but Victoria put a hand on her arm.

'Father looks so much older. Is he all right? Was the heart attack worse than you said?'

Her mother smiled. 'Don't worry so, Victoria. He has lost weight, and his hair is no longer black, but don't forget he's seventy now. And what's been going on at home has really shaken him; to see Indians killing Indians in that way is horrible. The politicians hoped India would be a secular state, that religion could be put to one side, but it has not proved to be the case.' She smiled, putting her arm around her waist.

'That's why we're here; I'm sure that away from all the stress and worry he'll soon recover the weight he's lost.'

Victoria wasn't convinced. Was her mother deluding herself? Her medical training told her there was something seriously wrong. Well, today wasn't the time to worry about it. She was so pleased to have them under her roof, to be able to share her children with them, that she would push her doubts aside until a more appropriate time.

She was tucking Junior into bed that evening when he said sleepily, 'Grandpa says he's not a king any more, that there are no kings in India. It's a public now. What's a public, Mummy?'

Victoria kissed him. 'A republic is where they don't have a king, queen or any royal family; it's where ordinary people choose who's going to run the country.' She thought this was a poor explanation, but it was enough to satisfy her son, after all not many three-year-olds would even ask such a question.

She went across to the matching bed where Jack put his arms round her neck and kissed her noisily. 'I like my grandma and grandpa, Mummy, but I wish my daddy in the picture was here as well; then it would be really lovely.'

Victoria's heart twisted and her eyes filled. 'I know, darling, I've told you your daddy loves you very much. I've shown you the money he sends that I put in the bank, but he lives in New York and finds it too far to come at the moment. I'm sure he will be over in England one day and maybe we will be a family with a daddy in it. Night, boys, love you. God bless. See you in the morning.'

When they said their prayers the boys always asked God to bless their daddy even though Lydia and Jack had never met him and Junior didn't remember him. Junior's real birthday was the following week, 14th April, but she'd decided to celebrate the boys' birthday at the end of May as this was halfway between their actual birthdates. Both of them thought they were born on May 31st.

She was already worrying what forms she would have to complete when they started school. Would she have to put their actual birthdates or add more lies? Life was so complicated. What had seemed like a simple idea when they were tiny was rapidly becoming a problem. Officialdom, in the form of the new National Health Service, which was starting, was demanding she fill in all of their details in order to register them on the system.

* * *

After two weeks, it was clear her parents were quite content to be living in more modest circumstances.

Her father had discovered how close Lord's was and was intending to watch the opening test match between England and Australia. He'd told her that Don Bradman was playing his last match, but this meant nothing to her. However, seeing him so enthusiastic meant a lot.

The weather continued warm and sunny and they all strolled to Regent's Park most mornings where the children fed the ducks and played on the swings, and if they were lucky got rowed on the boating lake. After lunch Lydia took a nap and the boys settled down to learning their letters, reading or other quiet pursuits.

The remainder of the afternoon was spent playing games in the garden and then it was teatime. The days slipped past and she was surprised neither of her parents expressed any wish to visit the sights of London. They had been with her for more than two weeks, but so smoothly had they fitted into her relaxed regime, that it seemed as though they'd been there forever.

Things were helped by the fact they had their own space on the other side of the house. When the conversion had been done the second stairs had been left in place, and the door that linked the houses upstairs could be firmly shut, giving her parents total privacy and much-needed peace. They were able to escape from the children whenever they felt the inclination. Since Anita had left Ada had taken over in the kitchen and produced plain but tasty meals, making not very much seem a lot more.

The children were fast asleep, exhausted by a

rowdy game of cricket, and the evening meal had been cleared away. Ada and Bert retired to their own accommodation, leaving Victoria to sit in her comfortable living room with her parents. They'd listened to the news, and were settled as if they'd spent the last two years living in St John's Wood together, not the last two weeks.

She smiled. It was strange how their roles were reversed – now she was looking after them, and she liked it that way. She thanked God she'd been given the opportunity to be with her parents, knowing if Henry had lived, she probably would never have seen them again.

'There's something I need to tell you. It's been eating me up and I think now's the right time.'

Her mother put down the magazine she was reading and her father folded *The Times* neatly and put it on the coffee table beside him. They both looked attentive, but didn't speak. She closed her eyes, trying to find the words that would make what she'd done seem less awful, more acceptable.

With a rush the story poured out. She told them about Amelia, how she'd been abandoned in Essex with her grandparents and how it was eating away at her, not being able to see her daughter, not having her with her. When she'd finished she raised her head to see her mother dabbing her eyes with a lace-edged handkerchief and her father blowing his nose discreetly.

'I'm so sorry. Amelia is your first grandchild – I shouldn't have done it.'

'No, you had every right, Victoria. It was your decision, and however hard it was, I think, in the circumstances, it was not only the correct one, it was courageous.' Her father cleared his throat. 'In fact, my dear, I am surprised you are as contented as you appear with all the turmoil and heartache you have had to endure in your short life. You're a strong young woman, and I'm proud of you.' Victoria looked at her mother, waiting to hear what she thought.

'I agree with your father, my love. Sometimes you have to do difficult things, and you do them because you love your child and for no other reason.'

Her mother was referring to the time she had almost died from grief at being parted from Henry. Her parents had been forced to give her up in the same way she'd given up Amelia. Her mother continued softly. 'Leaving your daughter with her grandparents, who were still grieving the loss of their only son, was the right thing to do, but I think now you're established in England maybe you could think about making contact again.'

Victoria swallowed. 'I've been thinking of nothing else, but the more I think about it the harder it becomes. She'll be eight years old now. For the past four years she's thought her mother has abandoned her. Why should she want to see me? I doubt Marion and Arthur would be happy to have me interfering after so long. I gave them guardianship, you know. I have no legal rights now.'

She wiped her eyes angrily. 'I've been sending letters to be put in a box at my solicitors. They will give it to her when she's twenty-one. Every birthday and Christmas, and sometimes in between, I've written to her, telling her how much I love her, telling her... well just everything that's been going on in our lives. What about my other children? How do I explain they have an older sister they knew nothing about?'

'I know it will be difficult, but they're young. The excitement of having an older sister would make up for not knowing her until now,' her mother said.

'There is a problem, Victoria. You are already enmeshed in a web of lies; I was never sure how wise it was pretending Jack and Junior are twins, even giving them a false birthday; however pure your motives, I can only see it ending in disaster.'

'What else could I do, Papa? I could have sent him

away, given Anita money, left her to bring up Jack by herself. Would that have been better for all of them?'

Her mother looked worried. She didn't like raised voices. 'Now, both of you, please don't start arguing. I've just learnt some incredible news. Let's sit and celebrate that, not worry about anything else tonight.'

Immediately she understood. Her father wasn't to be upset; he wasn't well enough. She got up and went over to his chair, taking his hands in hers. 'I'm sorry, but you're quite right. That's another reason I'm not going to contact Amelia just yet. I've got to decide how and when I'm going to tell the children.' She paused, not sure if now was the time to tell her parents what she had in mind. She decided it was.

'I'm going to try and contact Taylor. I still love him you know. I've always loved him, and forgave him a long time ago. He's not perfect, far from it, but I think as soon as I realised he was just a man like any other I wanted him back in my life. He really loved Junior, and I know he would love his other children too.'

'I can't believe you have had the strength to overlook his infidelity, his leaving you to fend for yourselves, his not coming to see his daughter...'

'Mother, I know all that – but look at me, look at all the lies I've told him. There's fault on both sides.'

Her father's hand was stroking her hair, as he'd

used to when she was a little girl, and she rested her head on his lap, feeling secure and comforted by his presence.

'I agree with you; Taylor is the father of your children and he should be here sharing their lives. Do you know where he is at the moment?'

She sat back, leaning against his chair so she could still feel the warmth of his legs against her side. 'I don't know exactly how to find him but he can be contacted through his lawyer or his agent. Any letters should reach him. I shall write tomorrow and with any luck he will respond quickly and then at last I can begin to unravel the lies I've lived with for so long.'

She got up early, before the children surfaced and demanded her attention, and went to sit at the table in the window that overlooked the back garden. This was where she wrote her journal and her correspondence. She took a large sheet of airmail paper, hating its thinness, wishing she could write on the thick Basildon Bond she used for internal mail. What she wanted to say should be on robust paper, not this pale blue, translucent stuff. It made her words seem less important.

She had spent a restless night trying to think how to phrase this letter, and in the end decided to keep it friendly and vague. She didn't mention Jack, or her parents, just said that if he was in England she would like them to meet, that it was time to put the past behind them.

She would explain everything if he responded positively. Of course, Taylor might not feel the same way about her any more – indeed, he might just be waiting to hear from her so he could ask for a divorce. She prayed this would not be the situation as the more she thought about it, the more she was sure she wanted to try again. This was not just for the children's sake, but also for her own.

She took the letter to the post office on the way to the park and her heart soared as she watched it disappear into the sack behind the counter. Perhaps in a few weeks' time Taylor would turn up at her door.

She stopped, her heart racing. She couldn't wait to see him again. When he did come, if he did, it would take a lot of explaining and compromising before they could start again. She was determined to tell him everything, about her parents – well – she could hardly avoid that as they were living with her, but also about Amelia. He had to accept what she'd done, forgive her as she had forgiven him, before they could move on and become a family.

15

COUNTRY LIVING?

For several weeks after the letter was posted Victoria waited eagerly each morning for the postman delivering down her cul-de-sac, but a reply from Taylor never arrived. As the summer days shortened into autumn she decided that he had made his position clear; by his silence he had told her that he didn't want to renew their relationship. She agonised over why he should have made this decision, believing maybe he'd met somebody else. After all, he'd jumped into bed with Anita scarcely six weeks after marrying her.

Her parents made no mention of returning to India; in fact as the days passed her father had become more robust, almost like his old self. He'd enjoyed the test matches but bemoaned the fact England had lost the series four–nil. He also watched almost every county game that had been played at Lord's. The boys had gone along with him a couple of times, with Bert for backup, and they had caught his passion for this strange three-day game that was incomprehensible to all but the cognoscenti.

Cricket bats were purchased, plus two sets of stumps and now, instead of ball throwing in the garden, there were games of cricket. Lydia was as eager to play as her brothers and, although still a toddler, she had excellent hand-to-eye coordination.

One evening at the end of September they were sitting on the brick terrace outside the French doors, drinking gin and tonic in the twilight, when Victoria realised she didn't want her parents to return to India. They were a family, even without Taylor and Amelia, and she was happier than she'd been for years. She was free to be herself, to acknowledge the past and look forward to the future.

She turned to her parents who were looking as relaxed and happy as she'd ever seen them. 'I've been thinking, why do you have to go back to India? Couldn't you stay here with us? You've got your own accommodation – there's plenty of room for us all here. When the boys start school I'm thinking of returning to work and unless I employ a nanny I shan't be able to. With you here, Mama, the children would hardly notice I was absent.'

She saw them exchange glances. 'My dear girl, we were about to ask you the same question. We have been so happy here in England; India is not the same since we left Marpur. If you're quite sure you wish to share your lives with us then we're absolutely certain we want to stay.

'If you do to go want to go back to work, darling, I should be absolutely thrilled to look after Lydia. She's adorable, and I can take the boys to and from school. I shall love having something purposeful to do again.'

Victoria looked from one to the other her eyes shining. 'I warn you it's cold and horrible here in the winter. We don't have monsoons, but we do have ice and snow and sometimes the sun doesn't shine for days.'

'Bert tells us the central heating in this house is very efficient and the shutters you added mean we are snug and draught-free, so we'll hardly notice the cold.'

She laughed. 'I think that's a bit of an exaggeration, Papa, but if you're prepared to brave the elements, then I'm absolutely thrilled. What a wonderful Christmas we'll have together this year.'

Her father grinned, an odd expression on his aristocratic face. 'Actually, my dear girl, I've got my eye on a rather nice motor car and, now we're going to be here permanently, I think I shall toddle along to the showroom tomorrow. I'll take Bert with me, and if you don't mind, I'll buy it. He rather fancies himself as a chauffeur; it seems he drove a tank in the army during the war so he's got plenty of experience.'

The laughter this comment caused fetched Ada from the kitchen. 'Did I hear my Bert mentioned then? What's he been up to now?'

'My father was telling me he's going to act as his chauffeur, and that he has every confidence that Bert having been a tank driver will have sufficient experience for this.'

Ada's chortle added to the merriment. 'Good Gawd! Don't think he's only driven tanks, Mrs King. He drove all sorts during the war. You'll be right as ninepence with him taking you around, sir.'

The magnificent Bentley arrived and Bert parked it on the short gravel driveway that led to what used to be a garage but was now his home. The car was his pride and joy; whenever he had a spare moment he was out there spitting and polishing. He also wore his new navy-blue jacket and gold braided cap at every opportunity, much to the children's delight. They thought he looked like the captain of a plane or liner, and before the weather got too cold for them to play outside, every afternoon he was often seen sitting on a chair pretending to sail across the ocean with the three children sitting behind him as passengers.

There wasn't a day when she didn't think about Amelia or Taylor, but she knew they were both out of her reach. She had to concentrate on what she had. The boys would be four next year and were due to start nursery school in September and she had done absolutely nothing about it. She dreaded facing a headmaster and having to lie about their ages so she was putting it off until the last possible moment.

Her mother had gently pointed out to her that if she left it any longer there might be no places in the school of their choice, but she ignored this advice and continued to bury her head firmly in the sand. The theatres were now open and they all went see *Cinderella* in the West End. The children were enthralled by the lights and music and laughter. The large Bentley was spacious enough to take them all. Ada, her mother and herself, with Lydia on one of their laps, sat on the commodious leather seat at the back. The two boys sat on the pull-down seats opposite, and her father travelled next to Bert in the front.

It amused Victoria to see how friendly her father and the handyman had become, they shared a love of cricket, expensive automobiles, and also her father had developed an interest in gardening. He had purchased a large greenhouse and had it attached to the house heating system. In it they were growing orchids, exotic plants and a fine crop of tomatoes.

On Christmas morning they all walked round to the St John the Baptist Church opposite the station. They came back to open the presents under the tree and eat a massive Christmas dinner. Ada's family in the country had done them proud – eggs and cream and a wonderful plump cockerel had arrived – and with the various exotica bought from Harrods and Fortnum & Mason's, they had more festive food than they could possibly eat.

The children had been ecstatic over the contents of the socks hung up on the mantelpiece overnight, and her parents intrigued, and not a little mystified, by the strange tradition of Father Christmas and his reindeer arriving overnight to fill the hosiery.

As usual Victoria said a silent prayer for her missing daughter, and also for her missing husband. She didn't know why he had rejected them, knew she ought to move on, start looking to the future without him, but she couldn't. Every time she looked at Jack especially, her heart was broken afresh. Most women would feel anger or bitterness, but what she felt was a dark void that could only be filled by his presence.

* * *

Sometime in January her father passed her a glossy journal folded open at the pages advertising expensive country properties. 'I rather thought, my dear, that I should purchase something in the country for us all. Keep this lovely little house in St John's Wood of course, and then in the cricket season I can come up here, but in the winter we can all be somewhere a little more congenial than London. What do you think of these properties? Bert and I have been investigating the area around Guildford. It's in Surrey, and it looks very promising.'

'So that's where you two have been when you disappear for hours in the Bentley. I was beginning to think you were up to something nefarious.'

He raised one aristocratic eyebrow and smiled slightly. 'Bert and I are above reproach, my dear.' He smiled and his eyes twinkled. 'However, I must admit occasionally we've stopped at a local hostelry and had a drink or two on the way home.'

She stared at the grand houses in the photographs. They were all far too large, reminded her of Marpur Palace, and she didn't want to go back to living in such grandeur. She rather liked the intimacy of the house she had. The first three houses were magnificent, but far too opulent. She noticed on the following page a picture of a small Georgian manor house, double-fronted, four beautifully proportioned shuttered windows on each side of an imposing porticoed front door. She fell in love with it immediately. It had extensive grounds of fifteen acres, including paddocks, stables and two self-contained cottages. She checked the address; the house was not far from Guildford, the town that her father had mentioned. It looked ideal.

'I like this. Have you been to see this one, Papa?'

He reached out and, taking the magazine back, looked at it with more interest. 'Actually, my dear, I haven't viewed any of them, just driven around, getting a feel for the place. The most important thing is, it's only a little over an hour's drive from here, so it's the perfect area for us to have a second home.'

Her mother came in and saw them looking at the adverts. 'Oh, so you've told Victoria our plans. What do you think, darling, would you like to have a home in the country as well as in London?'

'Yes, I think it would be far better for the children

to grow up surrounded by green fields. We could have ponies and dogs and so on. And I'm sure we can find them a good prep school in Guildford.'

'Excellent, that's settled. I shall contact the estate agents tomorrow and arrange for a viewing. Shall we all go down and see it or would you like Bert and I to look round first, check it out to make sure it has everything we want?'

'Well, as long as it's got plenty of bedrooms, we can put in any extra bathrooms and so on that we need. And this place has somewhere for Bert and Ada as well. What we really want to know is if there are suitable schools for the children.'

She was about to add 'and a hospital nearby where I can work', but she had abandoned the idea of working, at least for the moment. Immediately her father had mentioned buying a house in the country, not living full-time in London, she'd known that this was the right thing to do.

When Amelia eventually came to live with them they would need more rooms than they had here. At some time in the future she would write to Marion and Arthur and ask if she could go and see her daughter. That would be the first step; if she wasn't rejected by the little girl, they could start with afternoon visits, and perhaps Amelia would want to come and stay weekends and in the holidays. It wouldn't be quite the same as having her here all the time, but it would be so much better than nothing.

She tried to imagine what she looked like now. The last time she'd seen her she had been a mercurial four-year-old, blonde hair in pigtails, intelligent and independent, but no longer interested in a mummy who didn't live with her. She sighed. Her imaginings were an unlikely scenario. Her daughter had spent half her life without her. Why should she want to see her now?

* * *

Spring arrived again and her parents had now been living in St John's Wood for more than a year. The house near Guildford had proved to be perfect, but it had needed refurbishment. The central heating system was almost non-existent and they needed at least two more bathrooms, but apart from that it was faultless. Ada and Bert were absolutely thrilled with their new cottage; they had the large kitchen garden to look after and a pretty front garden to themselves. Ada would finally be able to have a cat, her animal of choice.

The purchase had gone through smoothly, the

deeds were transferred to her father's name, and the builders assured them they would be able to move in by June or July. Her mother and she had already started looking in the salerooms for suitable furniture, something fitting for a house of that period. They wanted antiques, Chippendale and early Victorian by preference.

She had spent several days visiting nursery schools in and around the Guildford area and had finally settled on Lanesborough, which seemed to have everything she needed. It was also the school in which the choristers from Guildford Cathedral were taught; this had to be a plus. She'd taken home the application forms, and they were sitting in an accusing pile on the table in her bedroom demanding her attention.

She had paid a year's fees in advance, in order to secure their places, but she still hadn't sent the necessary details. Filling in the form meant she was going to have to lie officially. She'd also avoided registering for the National Health Service that had been launched in the summer. None of them had needed medical attention, thank God.

The boys' official birthday was rapidly approaching and she decided to spend the afternoon in the West End buying their presents. Her parents had agreed to take the children to the Ritz for afternoon tea and they weren't expected back until bedtime.

The weather was warm so she was able to wear her latest acquisition, a Dior suit in moss green silk. The nipped-in waist of the jacket suited her. With her matching court shoes, kid gloves, handbag and the saucy hat, which was little more than a couple of small feathers and fitted perfectly over her chignon, she was confident she looked her best. She liked the new longer length, pencil-slim skirt; finally, the years of wartime austerity were beginning to ease, and the government had decided to let fashion have its way.

'You look lovely, my dear. It would be a shame for you to come home straightaway – dressed like that you should stay in the West End and catch a show.'

'I'm not sure I'd enjoy it on my own, Papa.'

'Even if you don't go to the theatre, you don't have to hurry back. Why not have a meal out – there are plenty of places a woman can go on her own without comment.'

They piled into the Bentley and Bert headed for Oxford Street. He parked neatly and hurried round to open the door and salute. To passers-by he looked as if he was driving royalty, his behaviour sent the children, on the back seat with their grandmother, into fits of giggles.

'Have a lovely time, and don't eat too much, and remember to keep your mouths closed when you chew.'

'Yes, Mummy,' chorused the three children.

'I think I might wander along Bond Street later and have a look in the galleries. We're going to need dozens of paintings to fill the blank walls, especially in the hallway and up the staircase. I know we bought a dozen or so assorted landscapes at the last auction, but I'd like something a little more modern.'

'As long as you don't want to buy one of that Picasso fellow's paintings, I don't mind what you get,' her father said cheerfully.

Bert pulled away smoothly and she waved as the car drove away. She appeared to be getting more than her fair share of admiring glances. It was a little after three o'clock so she decided to go to Hamleys, the toy shop, and have a browse around to see what she could find. There were more games and toys being made since the end of the war, and the factories were also importing from abroad again. She was hoping there would be a wider choice this year. She bought far too much and arranged for the gifts to be delivered the following week, gift-wrapped and labelled appropriately. Duty done, she stopped for a cup of tea before walking to Bond Street.

There were several prestigious galleries here amongst the smart dress shops and she hoped to discover the work of a new artist, someone she'd never heard of who painted the kind of landscapes she wanted. She knew she was hoping to find something like the semi-abstracts Taylor produced.

It was a little after six o'clock and ahead of her she saw expensive cars pulling up and disgorging well-dressed people onto the pavement. There must be a private viewing – she wondered who the artist was – whoever it was he was certainly attracting a prestigious crowd. There were also press photographers hanging around, their flashbulbs going off at regular intervals as another famous person stepped out.

She caught a glimpse of herself in a plate-glass window and knew she looked just as smart as any of the women going in, perhaps she could gate-crash, see for herself what all the fuss was about. She reached the entrance to the gallery in the street and froze. Her mouth dropped open, her eyes widened as staring down at her from a huge colour poster in the window was the face of her errant husband.

16

LOOSE ENDS

Taylor was in London and he hadn't bothered to contact her. She was tempted to walk past, harden her heart and ignore him the way he had callously ignored her these past years. But she couldn't. She'd slip in quietly, look at his paintings, perhaps buy one or two for the walls of their new home, and if she was lucky, she might catch a glimpse of him. She hoped that seeing him from a distance would cure her once and for all of her ridiculous devotion to his memory. The thought of his heart-stopping smile, floppy brown hair and wiry leanness sent her pulse racing in a ridiculous fashion.

She hesitated outside, watching the guests pausing at the door to show two uniformed doormen their engraved invitations. Well, that was that. If even the rich and famous needed verification they would hardly let a nonentity like her past.

She'd come so far that it would be silly to turn back. What was the worst that could happen? She would be politely sent on her way. Kismet would have spoken. She straightened the seams of her stockings, adjusted her hat, straightened her shoulders and glided gracefully to the door, expecting to be stopped.

The shorter of the two men was obviously about to ask for her invitation when the other one coughed loudly to attract his attention. She hesitated, waiting to be rejected but the doorman winked and then waved her in without asking to see an invitation. Puzzled, she walked inside to find the main gallery full of the fashionably dressed and well-spoken, all clutching glasses of wine and catalogues.

She walked to one side and stood in front of a massive seascape. How much Taylor had improved – this was the work of a master. She was not surprised to see the incredibly expensive canvas already had a neat red dot stuck on the label below the frame. She glanced along the row of similar paintings. They were all similarly adorned.

As she wandered about, drinking in the power of the paintings, knowing she was in the presence of a genius, she became aware that she was attracting a lot of unexplained attention. She wasn't the only woman on her own, so it couldn't be that. As she walked from painting to painting people were looking at her, half-smiling as if in recognition, and then glancing away to talk busily behind their catalogues.

There was an archway that led into the second, slightly smaller gallery, and that was equally busy. Perhaps Taylor was in there; it was worth having a look. Feeling decidedly uncomfortable at the many sideways glances, she almost retreated. She walked towards the archway and when she got there paused, unconsciously framing herself in this space, making her a focal point at that end of the room.

She glanced to one side and for a second time that evening her jaw dropped. The canvases in this room were portraits, and they were all of her – in battle-dress, in mufti, thankfully none in the nude, but all painted with such skill that it was as if she was looking at her reflection. He'd captured her expressions; he'd painted them with love. She looked to the far end of the room and there he was.

He was surrounded by a sycophantic group of people clutching notepads, obviously firing questions at him, and he was answering smoothly. He looked so different, more self-assured, bigger somehow, although she didn't think he'd actually grown. She stood; the room gradually falling silent as people became aware of her presence, realised this great artist's muse was in the room.

* * *

'Mr King, these portraits are your finest work. Why are they not for sale? You could ask thousands of dollars for them.'

Taylor ground his teeth. How many times did he have to answer the same damn question? He fixed a smile on his face. 'These paintings are of my wife. They're not for sale; they're for me.'

He glanced up and got the feeling that he was being watched, as though something cataclysmic was about to happen. He looked towards the end of the room and there, standing, breathtakingly beautiful, was the woman he thought of every waking moment and if he was lucky, dreamed about as well.

Jesus H. Christ, it was Victoria. Ignoring the reporters' outrage he shouldered his way through and ran down the length of the room feeling like Moses as the crowds parted to let him by. Why didn't she move? Why was she staring at him as if he was the last person she wanted to see? Then to his delight she started to move and suddenly she was running too and threw herself into his arms. For the first time since that horrible day three years ago he felt, just maybe, he had something to live for.

'Jesus, darling, I can't believe you're here.' He crushed her, lifting her from her feet, needing to feel every inch of her pressed against him. She was more substantial, had filled out, was more feminine, more lovely, more everything. 'Victoria, I've missed you so much. I love you. I can't believe you're here; I just can't believe it.'

She tilted her head and her eyes shone up at him, radiant with love. He closed the few inches between their mouths and kissed her. Initially his lips were soft, gentle, exploring the contours with his tongue, lost in the sensation, then he slid his hand round to cup the back of her head and deepened the kiss, drowning in her taste and touch.

Only when he felt the heat of flashbulbs going off in his face did he raise his head, his eyes glittering with tears. 'Christ! This is no good. We can't talk here, not with these parasites clocking our every move. Let's get out of here, honey.' She nodded, seemed as eager as he to leave the roomful of gawping spectators.

* * *

Victoria didn't care about the gaping crowds, the flashing lights; all she cared about was that he'd said he loved her, that he'd missed her. He wanted to take her away in order to talk to her. Then he took her hand and pulled her forward. He broke into the well-remembered military jog and she fell in beside him, laughing at the look of total stupefaction on the faces of the people he barged aside.

She heard the smash of breaking glass and knew their rapid departure was leaving chaos in its wake, but she didn't care. Outside he hailed a passing cab and when it ground to a halt they dashed across and he flung open the door and bundled her inside.

'Where to, guv?' the cabbie asked.

'The Savoy. I'm staying there. There's a lounge we can use, get a drink, coffee anything, somewhere we can be private and talk.'

Her throat felt dry. She did need a drink, but what she didn't need was to be hustled upstairs and into his bed. Once that happened it would be too late to tell him everything. She would be lost, back under his spell. If he rejected her after she told him she'd not recover a second time.

The taxi trundled into the turning circle in front of the Savoy and the uniformed doorman leapt down to open the door. Taylor handed the man a large, white five-pound note. 'Pay him and keep the change.'

His arm was firmly about her waist, as if he believed she might vanish at any moment, and she was hurried through the revolving door into the foyer. He headed straight for the reception desk and her heart sank.

'I'm not going to your room. Don't suggest it or I shall leave.'

'I'm not going to. I'm going to get my key, so then I can order drinks and so on and put it on my tab.'

Feeling foolish for having doubted his motives she flushed and he grinned at her embarrassment. With his key in his hand Taylor guided her expertly towards a secluded corner behind two potted aspidistras.

'Sit here, darling. What would you like to drink? Have you eaten?'

'No, I haven't. I'd like something long and non-alcoholic, orange juice perhaps, and sandwiches – as long as they don't have meat in them.'

'Back on the vegetarian diet? I don't eat meat any more either. It seemed to link us somehow. The places I've been the past few months it could have been anything – camel, monkey, dog – safer to stick to vegetables.'

She sat back in the chair, peeling off her gloves and placing them neatly over her handbag. A waiter hurried over to take his order, then Taylor turned and folded his long length into a chair beside her, his eyes questioning, his expression serious.

'I wanted to contact you but didn't know how to, so I thought if I held an exhibition here there was just a chance you'd read about it and seek me out.'

'Taylor, I wrote to you six months ago asking you to contact me. I sent a letter to Gus asking him to post it on, also to your lawyers in Boston. Surely you must have got one of them?'

His face became sad. 'I knew there were two letters, but I thought you were asking for a divorce, had met someone else, so I headed for South America; thought if I remained incommunicado, the letters would go away and I wouldn't have to read them.'

She looked at him. 'Incommunicado? No wonder you didn't get them. All these months I've been worrying that you didn't want to see me, and at the same time you were running away. What a lot of time we've wasted.'

The waiter returned bringing a trolley with immaculately presented sandwiches, a large pot of coffee, cups, saucers and plates and a cake stand laden with temptation. He also put down two glasses of freshly squeezed orange juice. Taylor waved him away, didn't even bother to sign the slip, and the man took the hint.

'I love you, Taylor; I've always loved you. I forgave you a long time ago for being unfaithful. It will always hurt, but it's in the past.' She paused. Now was the time to tell him everything, before he touched her again and made it even more difficult.

'No, please don't interrupt – there are things I have got to tell you, awful things, far worse than anything you've done to me and you need to know them before you decide if you want to come back into my life.' She looked at him, seeing nothing but love in his eyes. 'Whatever happens, Taylor, whatever you decide, promise me you'll still be a part of your children's lives? I don't want them to grow up not knowing their father, even if you don't want to be with me.'

He nodded, and seemed to be having difficulty speaking. 'I don't care what you've done. If you take me back, that's all I care about.'

'I hope that's true. I shall ask you again when I finish.' She drew a deep breath and started to tell him everything. She decided to start with who she was. She paused at the end of that first revelation to get his reaction.

'I don't give a flying fuck who you are, darling.' He

smiled, that slow melting smile and her insides flipped. 'It seems I married a real Brahmin – my parents would sure get a kick out of that.'

Reassured by his attitude to what she thought was the worst of her lies she told him about her daughter. This information seemed to affect him more than the other.

'Jesus, how could you have done that?'

She knew it. He thought leaving Amelia was unforgivable; she was going to lose him. But he continued, his eyes sparkling with tears. 'God, you're so brave; you left your parents for the man you loved, and then had to leave your baby so her grandparents were not left entirely on their own.'

'And you don't mind? The fact that I've been living a lie all these years, that I'm Anglo-Indian, that I have a nine-year-old daughter you knew nothing about?'

'I don't care if you have ten daughters – they'll all be welcome in my house. I love kids and it's been eating me up being apart from mine for so long.' He leant across and she thought he was going to pass her a sandwich but he pulled her closer and whispered in her ear.

'My room's upstairs; come up with me. I need to make love to you. I've thought of nothing else since I saw you this evening.' He made several other suggestions that made her blush but somehow she managed to resist.

'No, Taylor, I want you to think about this. Think of the implications. I don't want you to make a hasty decision. If you're going to come back, we're going to be a family; you've got to be able to accept that my parents will be living with us, and I hope one day Amelia will be with us as well. Can you deal with that?'

'I've already told you, honey, I don't care what you've done, who you are; what I care about is that we're back together, that you love me as much as I love you. I can't believe you've given me a second go. I can't think any other woman would do the same. I'll never be unfaithful again. In fact, you might not believe it, but there's been no one else since we parted.'

She wasn't sure she could believe it. Sex was such a big part of his life, but he wouldn't lie to her at this crucial point in their reconciliation.

'I believe you. There's been no one else in my life and if we can't be together, Taylor, there never will be. I'm still not coming upstairs with you. You've got to meet my parents, your children, and then we can think about bed.'

There was one last hurdle to pass. She wasn't sure how he'd react when he found Jack was being brought up as Junior's twin, and until she had seen his reaction, she wasn't going to commit herself. Once they'd made love it would be too late for her to turn back whatever he did or said.

He jumped to his feet. 'Stay here; have a sandwich. I'm going up to my room to pack. I'll pay and check out. Let me come back with you. I'll sleep in the spare room, but at least I'll be under the same roof as you. I'm never going to be away from you again if I can help it.'

She watched him thread his way between the hotel guests and vanish into the lift. She *was* hungry and the sandwiches did look tasty. She drank the orange juice and had eaten several triangles filled with cream cheese before he returned, battered holdall in his hand.

'Okay, I'm ready to go. I told the guy at the door to get a cab, but as you didn't tell me where you live I couldn't give him the address.'

'Scott Ellis Gardens, St John's Wood. It's next to Lord's Cricket Ground and a short walk to Regent's Park, perfect for the children.'

Taylor carefully put his bag between them; the tension was palpable. If he was feeling half the explosive desire she was, if they so much as brushed fingers they might give the cabbie a display on his back seat that would shock him to the core.

The lone street light was flickering outside the house, allowing them enough illumination to see their way to the front door. 'I expect my parents will have gone to bed by now. They live in the other half of the house and they always retire early.'

She saw Taylor raise his wrist in order see his watch face. 'It's a little after nine o'clock. There don't seem to be any downstairs lights on. I sure hope they've gone to bed. I'm going to see the children – after that I don't think I'll be in any fit state to meet my in-laws.'

They stepped into the entrance hall and it was quiet, certainly in her half of the house everyone was asleep. 'Will you bolt the door for me, Taylor? I'll go up and shut the communicating door. My parents will know I'm home and can then go to sleep without having to keep one ear out for the children.'

She didn't invite him to follow. She'd been thinking all the way back about how best to introduce him to his children and had decided it would be better if he did it on his own. She was going to wait downstairs – that way if he was shocked or revolted at finding his illegitimate son sharing the same room as Junior it would be easier for him to leave.

Upstairs she closed the door, then checked first on Lydia. Her daughter was sleeping sweetly, two fingers, as always, in her mouth and her rag doll firmly under her other arm. Victoria gently removed the fingers and straightened the covers. She left the door open and went through the communicating door to the boys' room.

Junior was sprawled across the bed, like a starfish on the beach, his pillow on the floor, his blankets scrunched under him. She lifted him and put him inside the sheets before crossing to check on Jack. He was a tidy sleeper, with one arm tucked under his pillow the other possessively around his golly.

When she came downstairs Taylor was at the bottom, his face questioning. 'I'm going to put the kettle on. We don't have an electric percolator. I'm sure you want something to eat. I noticed that you didn't touch the sandwiches. Go on up – I've left the children's rooms open. I'll be in the kitchen.'

She listened for his footsteps crossing Lydia's room, which was directly above her, but couldn't hear him through the thickness of the carpet. She fiddled around with the complicated percolator and began making a pile of cheese and pickle sandwiches. She glanced at the kitchen clock. It has been almost half an hour. How much longer was he going to be?

Then she heard him returning and braced herself. He walked in, his cheeks unashamedly wet, too choked to speak. He held out his arms and she walked in.

'How could you have done that? Taken in that little boy? I can't believe it – I didn't think I could love you any more, but you're just the most amazing woman. I never thought I would see the little guy again, but there he was, next to his brother. I still can't believe it.'

'And Lydia? What do you think of your daughter?'

'She's just so cute – she looks just like you, sweetheart. Did you know that?'

The percolator boiled dry and the sandwiches curled up on the plate. If her parents had chosen, as they sometimes did, to come down and make themselves a late-night cocoa they would have found her making love to her husband on the living room floor.

* * *

Taylor carried her up to bed and they made love twice more before falling asleep. He was woken by a slight sound at the door. He pushed himself up on one elbow and saw Junior staring back at him. His son vanished and he heard him whispering loudly to his brother.

'There's a strange man in bed with Mummy. Come and see, Jack.'

'Me too! me too!' Lydia squealed, who from the rhythmic creaking was bouncing up and down on her bed. The three children were at the door and peeked round; he closed his eyes, pretending to be asleep, giving them the chance to see who it was that had invaded their privacy. He heard pushing and shoving and then they'd gone. Jack's treble was raised above that of his siblings.

'That's not a strange man, you silly-billy, that's a *daddy*. Look at the daddy picture we have hanging on the wall.'

His heart squeezed and tears filled his eyes. Christ – he had cried more in the past twelve hours than he'd done in his entire life. He'd not shed a tear when Victoria had kicked him out as he'd been too numb. He couldn't believe his kids seemed ready to accept him, welcome him into their lives. He nudged his wife. 'Honey, we're about to get a visitation. The kids are coming in to join us.'

17

NO MORE LIES

Victoria sat up, deftly covering her naked breasts with the sheet before her three children erupted into the room and flung themselves on the bed. Normally she slept in a voluminous cotton nightie. The two boys wrestled with Taylor. Lydia hung back, fingers in her mouth, sitting in Victoria's arms, not quite sure about this strange man who looked vaguely familiar.

Taylor turned to her; his smile spoke for him. 'My boys are just great.' Settling one each side of him he reached out his hands to his daughter. She shook her head and shrunk back, still not sure. 'I'm your daddy, sweetheart. Won't you come and give me a hug like your big brothers?'

These were the magic words. Whatever her big

brothers did then Lydia wanted to copy. She launched herself across the bed and landed on his chest. Victoria watched him. He was in his element, a natural-born father. How could they both have been so stupid as to throw away these precious years?

Seeing his children close to him made her think of Amelia. It wasn't fair. He had all his children in spite of everything, but she was still missing one vital part of her family – the one thing that would make her life complete.

She saw him glance up at her and smile sympathetically; he understood, knew what she was thinking.

She smiled back and his hand left the group hug to take hers and carry it to his lips. Jack sat up. 'Look, Daddy's kissing Mummy's hand – that's disgusting.'

'Gusting! Gusting!' Lydia chanted gleefully.

Junior wriggled and appeared at the bottom of the bed, his face flushed and happy. 'I'm going to get dressed. I bet I can be dressed quicker than you, Jack.'

The children vanished into their own rooms and she could hear them arguing happily as they got into their clothes.

'What about the little one? Surely she can't dress herself?'

'No, but when the boys are ready they help her. I

have to make sure I leave out their clothes. You can imagine what they'd look like if they had a free choice.'

He chuckled 'The boys are great and really wonderful with her. I don't think Junior would have been so accepting of a baby sister if he hadn't learnt to share with Jack. Do you have a shower here? Or do I have to use the tub?'

'No, I had a shower put in. It's through there; the door's ajar. You go first, then when you're dressed, I'll shower.'

Her parents took Taylor's unexpected arrival in their stride; they liked him immediately and could see how happy she was. Even if they'd hated him, they would have welcomed him into the family.

He had to go back to the gallery, to apologise to Gus and the gallery owner for his sudden departure the previous night. He wanted her to come with him, didn't want to be away from her for an instant, but she declined, thinking it would be better to stay where she was and answer any questions the children had.

The Times flopped onto the doormat and Victoria brought it into her father. The house looked no different but everything had changed. She felt as though she was floating several inches above the floor, and the children kept giggling and laughing and the word 'daddy' was mentioned so many times she was beginning to be sick of the sound of it. Her father suddenly coughed, spraying coffee over his immaculate white shirt.

Instantly Victoria hurried over, worried he was having some sort of spasm.

'Look at this. My God, Victoria, have you no sense of decorum?' She looked, and to her horror there was a photograph of her, feet dangling in the air, being thoroughly kissed by Taylor. The headline said it all. 'The King Reunited With His Queen'. She laughed; she wasn't going to apologise.

'I'm sorry if you're offended, Papa, but we both forgot where we were. That was the best moment of my life, even better than the day we got married.'

He nodded, apparently satisfied with her answer. He stood up tossing the newspaper to one side as if it was contaminated. 'I have to go and change my shirt. Don't let your mother see that; she'd be deeply shocked.'

The next day Taylor happened to notice the pile of official-looking forms lying on the table in their bedroom. 'What's all this, honey?'

'It's the boys' prep school forms and we're supposed to register with a GP but I can't bring myself to lie and I don't know how to tell the boys. I'm not sure that they'd understand.' Taylor knew about changing the boys' birthday to the end of May.

'Fill them in. Who the hell cares what day it is? When they find out, the boys will be adults and it won't matter. Toss me over a pen and I'll do it for you. I'm their father after all. Won't they expect me to sign the papers?'

'I hadn't thought of that. Yes, I'd much rather you did it. I decided I want no more lies in my life. But of course you can lie as much you like, as long as I don't have to.'

He grinned, his eyes full of affection. 'This is the only lie I'm going to tell – as far as we and the rest of the world are concerned Junior and Jack are twins and their birthday's May 31st. They don't need to know until they grow up. Forget about it, darling.'

* * *

He watched his wife's face. He knew exactly what she was thinking. There was still one lie she hadn't unravelled, one loose end she hadn't tied. She'd given him everything, given him Jack, the son he thought he'd never see again, and he was going to return the favour. After breakfast he found his father-in-law.

'Excuse me, sir, can I borrow the Bentley? I don't

need Bert, I'll drive myself. There's something I need to do.'

He saw the man's appraising gaze, and then he nodded. 'Of course, you can, young man. The keys are hanging by the back door; it has a tank full of fuel. I'm afraid it's rather heavy on petrol. You might need to get some more if your journey is long.' He didn't ask directly where he was going and Taylor didn't tell him.

Victoria was out with the children and Mrs Bahani. They'd gone to the park to feed the ducks and play on the swings. He went into the kitchen where Ada, the housekeeper, was washing up.

'Ada, I'm going out. I should be back mid-afternoon. Can you tell Mrs King for me?'

The place he was looking for was called 'The Rookery', and was in a little village called Mountnessing, near Ingatestone in Essex. He'd looked it up and knew exactly where to go.

He pulled onto the sweeping drive just after noon and found the front door wide open, but no one around. After parking the car, he climbed out and stretched to relieve the cramp in his legs. It had taken him longer to find this godforsaken neck of the woods than he'd anticipated.

He could hear the sound of voices from the back of the house and decided to walk round and investigate. The house was enormous, probably as big as the one his father-in-law had purchased in Surrey; he hadn't seen that yet, but was looking forward to visiting soon. On the lawn he saw a little girl, her long braided hair flying out behind her, being pushed on a swing by an elderly grey-haired gentleman, who seemed to be finding the exertion an effort.

'Hi there, I'm sorry to disturb you, but are you Arthur Hindley-Jones?'

The old man looked up, a questioning expression on his face. 'I certainly am, and who might you be?'

The girl had her back to him, so he couldn't see her face. 'Taylor King, sir. I'm married to your former daughter-in-law, Victoria Hindley-Jones.'

Hearing the name *Victoria* the girl flung herself from the swing and turned round, holding onto the rope as if for support. He couldn't believe it; this child was the image of his darling wife, only with cornflower blue eyes.

'Hi, honey, you must be Amelia. I've sure heard a lot about you.'

The child recovered her composure and releasing the swing stepped away from her grandfather, which surprised Taylor, and walked towards him. Everything, from the tilt of the head, to the lightness of her footsteps, reminded him of Victoria.

'You said you're married to Victoria Hindley-Jones? Does that mean you're married to my mummy? That you're my stepfather?'

He dropped down to his haunches, bringing his eyes level with hers. 'It sure does, honey. I've got to tell you, your mommy's missed you every minute of every day. She'd really like to see you, if your grandpa and grandma would let you come.'

The child's smile pierced his heart. The longing on her face told him he'd made the right decision to come. She turned to her grandfather. 'I can go, can't I, Grandfather? I know you and Grandma find me rather tiresome at times. I heard you talking about it and I'm sure you would prefer not to have me bouncing about the house all the time.'

The old man smiled lovingly at his granddaughter. 'We didn't mean you to hear that, poppet. You know we love you absolutely, but we also know how desperately you want to see your mother again.' He glanced at Taylor before finishing his sentence. 'Since Nanny died it's been difficult for all of us.' Taylor regained his feet and turned to Mr Hindley-Jones who had been watching this exchange with interest.

'Well, Mr King, come along in and have some lunch. Tell me all about Victoria, how's she been these past five years? And tell me about yourself. You are an

American, but I can't quite place the state you come from.'

Inside he met Mrs Hindley-Jones, a cheerful lady, but tired-looking. It soon became apparent the care of their grandchild had rested entirely with the elderly nanny and when she'd died the previous year they'd had to take over things, and it had become too much for them.

Amelia went to collect some drawings to show him; she'd been fascinated to discover her new father was a famous artist and wanted to fetch her own paintings immediately to hear his opinion.

'Victoria has been sending letters, birthday cards, Christmas cards and gifts to her lawyers every birthday and Christmas. She left Amelia with you because she thought you needed her more than she did. Now we're settled, we have three children of our own, we'd really like to have her living with us. Is that possible?'

They exchanged such looks of relief he already knew their answer would be yes. 'Possible? Young man, you're the answer to our prayers. We had decided to send our darling away to school this September. She's just too much for a pair of old folks like us. We never thought we'd hear from Victoria again. Amelia's so intelligent and lively and she desperately needs younger company.'

His wife blew her nose loudly. 'We loved – love Victoria – she made our boy so happy. Take Amelia with you today. It won't take long to pack a few things. Bring Victoria and your other children down for Sunday lunch. We would really like to see her again, as she was like a daughter to us and we've missed her dreadfully since she left.'

Taylor felt his throat thicken and he cleared it noisily. 'I will, sir, ma'am – it'll be our pleasure. I have to tell you that there are one or two other things you need to know before we come down.'

He quickly filled them in on Victoria's ancestry and instead of being horrified they were amazed that a girl as young as Victoria had been – seventeen years old – had been prepared to give up her heritage, her home and family in order to be with their son.

With his new daughter settled beside him, her favourite bear clutched in her arms, her eyes shining with excitement and happiness, he drove off immediately after lunch. He had arranged they would return at midday the following Sunday, and would collect the trunk with the rest of her belongings then.

He looked down at the child beside him and his heart filled with love. He'd wondered, as he'd driven down to Essex, whether he would feel the same about someone else's child, but she looked so like her mother he loved her already.

'I haven't told your mommy I'm fetching you, so you'll be a big surprise for her.'

The child's smile faltered. 'Do you think she'll want to see me? I know you said she'd been sending me letters, but I've never seen them.'

'I'll get in touch with the lawyers tomorrow and get that box brought to you, then you can sit and read them together.' For the rest of the journey Amelia asked question after question about her two brothers and baby sister. She was equally fascinated about her Indian grandparents, and a little disappointed to find they no longer wore the costume of their home country.

He parked the car neatly in the short drive and went around to open the door in order to let Amelia out. He could hear his family in the garden. He stopped to listen. Yes – all three children were out there with their grandparents. This meant Victoria could meet her daughter without an audience.

He had his own key so didn't need to ring the bell. They stepped into the hall and he could hear Victoria talking to Ada in the kitchen. Pushing the door closed quietly, he put his finger on his lips and moved the child out of sight behind him. He dropped the suitcase behind the hat stand.

'Darling, I'm back, and I've brought a surprise for you.' She appeared in the kitchen door, her lips curved in a smile of welcome that brought tears to his eyes.

'We wondered where you'd been. Papa said you had an errand to run. What have you brought me? I hope it's something special.'

Like a magician he reached behind him and guided the child to stand between his arms and face her mother for the first time in five years. He watched Victoria's face pale and for moment she swayed; he thought she was going to faint. Then she dropped to her knees and holding her arms open, tears streaming down her face, said softly, 'Amelia, my darling baby. I'm your mummy. Do you remember me?'

The little girl launched herself like a bullet and he stood by watching them crying in each other's arms and knew, finally, the woman he loved more than his life, was no longer living under a shadow.

ABOUT THE AUTHOR

Fenella J. Miller is a bestselling writer of historical sagas. She also has a passion for Regency romantic adventures and has published over fifty to great acclaim.

Sign up to Fenella J. Miller's mailing list for news, competitions and updates on future books.

Visit Fenella's website: www.fenellajmiller.co.uk

Follow Fenella on social media here:

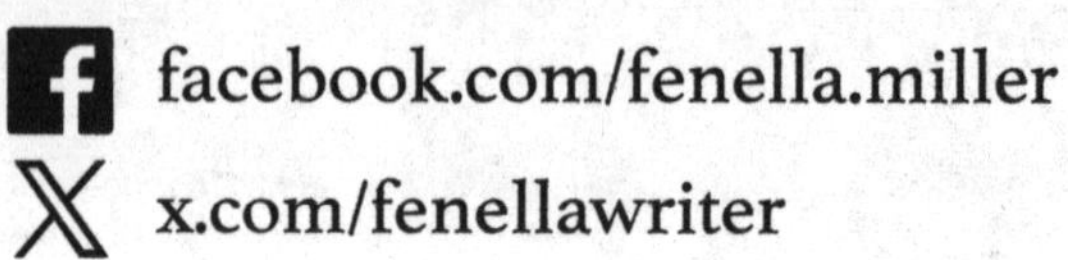

facebook.com/fenella.miller

x.com/fenellawriter

ALSO BY FENELLA J MILLER

Goodwill House Series

The War Girls of Goodwill House

New Recruits at Goodwill House

Duty Calls at Goodwill House

The Land Girls of Goodwill House

A Wartime Reunion at Goodwill House

Wedding Bells at Goodwill House

A Christmas Baby at Goodwill House

The Army Girls Series

Army Girls: Reporting For Duty

Army Girls: Heartbreak and Hope

Army Girls: Behind the Guns

The Pilot's Girl Series

The Pilot's Girl

A Wedding for the Pilot's Girl

A Dilemma for the Pilot's Girl

A Second Chance for the Pilot's Girl

Victoria's War Series

The Nurse's War

The Nurse's Homecoming

Standalone

The Land Girl's Secret

The Pilot's Story

www.ingramcontent.com/pod-product-compliance
Lightning Source LLC
LaVergne TN
LVHW030914080826
845145LV00012B/2890

* 9 7 8 1 8 3 5 1 8 6 7 3 2 *